GHOST WORKS

Daphne Marlatt

NeWest

Canadian Cataloguing in Publication Data

Marlatt, Daphne, 1942-
    Ghost works

Contents: Zócalo—How hug a stone—Month of hungry ghosts.

    I. Title.
PS8576.A74G5 1993   C813'.54   C93-091176-8
PR9199.3.M37G5 1993

Credits
Editor for the Press: Smaro Kamboureli
Cover design: Diane Jensen
Cover photo: Perry Low
Interior design: John Luckhurst/GDL

Financial assistance: NeWest Press gratefully acknowledges the financial assistance of The Canada Council; The Alberta Foundation for the Arts, a beneficiary of the Lottery Fund of the Government of Alberta; and The NeWest Institute for Western Canadian Studies.

Printed and bound in Canada by Hignell Printing Limited.

NeWest Publishers Limited
Suite 310, 10359 - 82 Avenue
Edmonton, Alberta T6E 1Z9

CONTENTS

GHOST WORKS

PREFACE

Ghost Works. Well, why ghost? assuming these texts are not ghost-written, as indeed they are not—unless we take the muse to be some sort of ghost, for like a ghost she comes and goes. Musings they are, travel musings, written out of three trips to three different countries. Each time, i travelled in the company of different others but always, it turned out, in the company of my mother who had died in 1975, a few months before that first journey. Each work struggles with the notion of here, what being here means, what it includes or excludes. At first feared, then embraced, mother/other (where) become muse.

My New Year's trip with my then-partner to the Yucatan in Mexico, a culture where death is very present, was prefaced by a dream that March before my mother's death and closed with a dream-visit to her in the underworld. On the second journey, in the month of her death a year later, my sister and i accompanied our father in our mother's stead on a trip that had been planned as their last one back to Penang, where they began their married life and where we had lived as children. Our visit coincided with the Chinese festival month of Hungry Ghosts when the ghosts of the inadequately remembered dead return to haunt the world of the living. The last journey, five years later, was to England, always referred to by my parents as "home" though neither of them had lived there since the Thirties. I took my son to what was then the ghost of a home, to visit his great-grand-mother and great-uncle and family, relatives he had never seen. I took with me the words of the English medium i visited in Vancouver who relived my mother's death and brought me messages from her.

None of this is fiction, though it may be (and *Zócalo* certainly has been) read as such. Autobiography would seem to occupy the opposite end of the spectrum from ghost-writing. Not the writing of someone standing in for someone else, but writing in your own *stead*, i mean listening to and writing the movements of your story, their strange patterns, their forward-and-back that form the *place* you recognize yourself in—you/i—a place occupied not by one but many selves, a place full of ghosts, those visitants from previous and other ways of being. As such this writing probes the house of the self, haunting its narrow construction, breaking down its oh-so-edified walls. After all, place was once a broad street, thronged with who knows who.

Perhaps this is an immigrant's preoccupation. Or a border-crosser's. Or a genre/gender crosser's (if autobiography can be seen as divorced from poetry—that muse again, or lesbianism divorced from heterosexuality—that haunting family). Heterogenous, this place here, so overlaid with other places: this self here sieved through with other selves when there was here and you were, you are, me.

For a woman writing autobiography, history itself becomes a ghost, one that is always disappearing only to reappear on the page ahead. Collective *and* personal. Because she forgets herself, she loses herself in this or that, or finds herself wiped out, erased from her place in history, even her personal history. Because, so many becauses, but one of them revolves around her eclipsed mother whose shadow she has difficulty escaping—because her mother didn't or couldn't from hers, because this fraught relationship has yet to receive the attention it deserves. The abdication of the mother, of all the mothers, who were abandoned in their turn. And so we keep reinventing ourselves, without models (or so we think). Our histories ghostly. And ghosts, who are hungry for recognition as we know, return, return . . . .

Daphne Marlatt
Saltspring 1993

have to be more honest? but perhaps there's the comfort of knowing the same diffs?

ZÓCALO

for Roy

Among the Aztecs, dream interpretation and
divination by dreams were the prerogative of the
priestly class 'teopexqui,' the Masters of the Secret
Things; and among the Maya of 'cocome,'
the Listeners.

Dreams: *Visions of the Night*

→ they don't know how they know each other
  "   "   "   "   "   "   others
  "   "   "   "   "   cd " the others' past
  she doesn't know how she knows herself.
— commt idear are — no Mayan

— reading the light in people's eyes.
  "   "   "   "   in landscape

existential
→ he doesn't make it much easier for her
or if we did it would distort
— have a community of the body — a lot of worms
gone round So arms not going around
→ is it easier for women or all dealing w similar
distortions — or more diffs.

JOURNEY

They had come from elsewhere, hundreds of them. Now they are stopped in a line that curves back down the road in the fading light. She can see his white truck glimmering behind her, and behind him, these cars, these trucks and jeeps and vans, sprawling into dark. Now they are here, now she sees the actual lineup, sees she is in it, she feels they have been pulled here, through a vast network of highways, roads, to this, this centre (as if it were the heart of a continent, it isn't), this inspection centre—yes, isn't that why they have come? the vehicles, their mechanism requiring inspection.

She takes her foot off the clutch and rolls down the window. After flying through the passes of those hills and then what seemed to be growing desert, though here, yes, there are trees, but stunted and far apart—it's hard to adjust to a crawl, her body, the car even, still canted forward in the impetus of speed, flying, it felt like flying, both windows down, hair streaming in the stream of air brushing her eyes trying to gauge, by feel, the lengths to leave according to their speed, his truck and her car juggling position in a kind of follow the leader or, since both love speed, a kind of dare, contingent on the bends, the turns, and then, after the tension of thrusting ahead, letting her foot relax on the pedal, slipping back, feeling the slippage of air over the body of her car which responds like some animal alive to pavement its wheels mediate. Surrounding country, then, was just a blur.

And now she is here, is in it, rolls down the window and night comes in, just the beginning edges of it dawning (how can that be?—but nothing seems to end here, sun glimmers horizontal and dusty behind those hills, as it has for the past hour, caught, on the verge of going—only not, only night bent on presence, invisibly growing.

And are they stopped? It seems to be something between first gear and none, or out of, slipping the clutch. Of course they're moving up a slight incline. Let the car ahead gain a few feet so at least she can *move* then, instead of slipping the clutch. She misses their game and thinks he'll wonder what is holding them up. Glancing in the mirror for *him* now, and not the truck, she finds him a yard or so behind, arms crossed on the wheel and glancing out the side window. What's he looking at?

Rolls down hers, sees dust has stopped for the most part, just a light density in air, powder soft. Of course the earth here's sandy, or, she can't tell by colour, it's getting dark, it feels in the air, on the skin like a fine pulverized dirt, inland and old. The sea beyond those hills, quite a long way beyond—was it yesterday? But there's a kind of freshness here she hasn't sensed before, not fresh, no, something out of night falling, some bush or herb that, freshened by the drop in temperature, releases an odour that is acrid and sweet.

She glances back at the truck, turning her head to look over her shoulder through the rear window. His window is dusty, he has the wipers going, squirting a clear arc to see through. She waves her hand to break his focus. He sees her and waves back and she turns forward, feeling a smile on her own face. Sees the car ahead has moved several yards. Shifts quickly into gear and follows. The smile, once she has felt it, begins to fade—it seems absurd to be smiling at a long line of cars— but she feels his presence warm behind her head like hair.

Near the top of the incline all the cars bear signs as if they had been numbered. She assumes she also has one and sees, glancing back, that he does too, but she doesn't remember seeing any men or feeling anyone approach the car. Maybe the signs have suction cups that would have been silently attached? Though she stares hard at the car ahead—actually it's a

truck and, now that she stares intently, seems to be in some way
official, a patrol truck, the kind a road construction crew uses to lead a
line of cars through a restricted area—she cannot make out how the
sign sticks. Each sign bears a number and a line or two of print too
small to read. Not even the letters look recognizable and she thinks
perhaps it's in some native language.

But now the truck in front, what is
it doing? backs up a bit, turning, leaves the line and heads off down the
road. Its brake lights flash on, pause, it is waiting—for her? Is she
supposed to follow? If it's a patrol truck maybe it's starting a new lineup
closer in to town, just to speed things up. She glances through the
mirror, behind, to him, but can't make out whether he signals she
should go or not. The patrol truck is still waiting, lights above and
beside its sign flashing number seven. She's the next one, no one can
move if she doesn't. She releases the clutch, steps on the pedal and
veers out.

Her guide begins to pick up speed and she can see an unac-
countable bend coming up. She glances back—is he following in the
white truck?—but finds herself simultaneously at the bend before she
can see—she *thought* she saw something white, but her attention is
taken up with manoeuvering the turn at high speed. Out in the open,
now they have left the avenue and moved into open country, the truck
is streaking down the road. She presses hard on the pedal trying to
catch up but the distance lengthens. Is it trying to lose her? Should she
have followed? She remembers getting out of the car to look at her
sign. Was it number six? (at least she thinks she remembers) was it
number nine? Yes, she had to fix it with the print so she could tell—it
was number six. If the truck is number seven she must obviously follow
it. But was it really part of the line? She sees in the growing distance a
number of tail-dragging black sedans, she can almost hear shouts, dogs
barking, can almost see the sedans full of people, kids. So it's a native
truck, it has nothing to do with the line. But it must know where to go,
it must be going somewhere. The dust it leaves fills up the road.
Impossible, impossible to see. She comes to a halt beside a ditch filled

with dry weeds, fencepost above, a field. No one else on the road. A creeping stillness that is twilight glimmers down its length.

She gets out and stands alone for some time. No one, nothing comes. The pavement through the soles of her runners where heat is trapped around her feet, a sweat that is even now turning cold in the cool of evening, the pavement feels smooth, hardly tangible. She moves off toward the edge where weeds are and dirt. Her walking has slowed to an effort through air thick with smells of, what, some kind of dry grass smoke. Distance is charged with it. A faint magnetism runs between things, the fencepost and her feet, this stalk and that. No moon? She has turned, intending the full horizon, but finds herself looking west to the hills light still flares behind.

She will go in, there is a driveway further back, much overgrown, she will go in and ask.

Their faces hang in the dusk like fruit off a tree. She is standing on their land talking to them. On her left the man bends slightly over a stick or the handle of a pitchfork. To her right the two women and the girl—their faces float up towards her in the dusk, hardly aware, it seems, of what she sees as startling: daughter, mother, grandmother clustered together like so many berries on the one bush—all staring, simply, at her own white face.

It was number seven, she says, the truck, where would a number seven truck be going? You see, I'm number six and I was supposed to be following . . . and then she hesitates. If she is six, shouldn't the truck have been number five since it was ahead of her? She remembers the number seven, seven, flashing in the light. But how could that be?

In the stillness they watch her face. Something is gathering in the air, something she can't see. 'Strange things . . . ' He seems reluctant to go on, and she turns to the woman she imagines might speak out of sympathy. What does he mean?

The woman doesn't answer. Or rather, behind her a fencepost

comes into view, bearing something nailed to it, some flayed animal. Its tawny hide flares up in the halflight. Matted fur. A warning? She thinks, that skin was nailed there for someone to see.

'I will tell you now is the time, now, when man's powers are coming to the full . . . ' It is pronounced, not spoken personally, not spoken to her at all. And yet she is allowed to overhear.

What do you mean? Is that all she can say? In the pressure of their silence she feels they feel she must know and is only pretending ignorance.

'The power of the sea and the power of dwarfs are acting together—that's what my mother would say.' She turns her head to the old woman but the woman continues staring at her without expression, without understanding.

Go back to the line, he says, we can't help you.

Walking back to the car she is walking *toward* the hills light is still fading behind. Time seems to press in from there, like some tide rising, like fear. He is right. They cannot help her.

Back in the car, she must turn around, but where? Drives on a little way, looking. There on the left, an abandoned garage, nailed shut, empty, and in front, a white truck. As she walks over to its window, she sees him in the passenger's seat, inert. For a second she thinks he is dead. What're you doing? Relief and fear sharpen her voice as he turns. He says quietly, I can't drive, and indicates the seat beside him. On it, a parcel trussed up in rope sits in front of the driver's wheel, bulkily in front, leaving no room for him.

I followed you when you first left the line, he says, I trusted your sense of direction. I thought you were following the sea.

Here? But then she remembers what was said. The parcel sits there, malevolent and unmoving. It almost emanates its own presence, not a sign but, more inexplicably, a knowledge of itself in front of them. She doesn't ask him how it got there.

We must go back.
Now.

She is driving and he is in her car. She is trying to explain that
there is no other way out but the way they came, that the country
surrounds them and there is very little room—only the thread of their
coming the way they came. They are still looking for a place to turn.
Up ahead, a stone wall on the right, and beyond it, a driveway. As the
wall approaches and runs beside them, he leans forward and she hears
him say, they knew how to depict expression, certainly—almost real.
Looking, she sees them rise up from the ground, a few lopsided crosses
among them, huge iron heads like jack-o-lanterns with holes for eyes
and nose, but the mouths, the mouths have teeth, lips, some with
tongues even, myriad expressions of laughter, or scorn, or knowing
smiles. As the car begins to pick up speed, she sees, their lips parted
slightly, they are breathing, these mouths, as they themselves are
turning into, a mistake, that driveway, carried by the momentum of a
plan, into the driveway of those others, those heads, too late, onto *their*
ground—No!—unwinds,

backward,

they are flying backward outside
time in open country, across fields, across terrain that slips under them
as they fly back in the slippage of their own coming, down the road,
through the house, wait, we can't just fly through their house,
through,

she sees him in a corner on a chair, unblinking, his stare
which hasn't left her face since she walked away, the man she asked
directions of, she sees he has known, he has always known, having just
removed the pipe, it is in his hand, it gleams in his eye which holds
hers as they fly by, just before and into the night, she realizes, looking
back, how small he is.

PROGRESO

New Year's Day, it turns out, is the day they go to Progreso, they go to the sea, to the light, to where they think sea light lies, eastward across that land stretching east & west (or so she thinks), under the sun's westward journey it lies like a great thumb sticking into the Caribbean, lies in fact north & south, & dry as a stone its new year begins at summer solstice when the rains come down. So to get to the sea they take a bus north, north, which is strange to them, who come from a north that lies east & west, where to get to the sea they go west, or east, but here they go north when the sun is furthest south, as if that might restore its northward journey, as once it might. But now the new year is Christ's they celebrate, leaving the zócalo where the xmas tree lights & the stone cathedral looms, leaving the real-painted faces of saints & virgin, the plaster body of Christ nailed to the cross, they take a bus away from the zócalo, leave the center of town with its benches & ahuatl trees, its shoeshine men or boys, its orange vendors, & go, out where the wind chases itself in an endless ring through dark shadows of bars, out to the white of the beach, the pier, the promenade, where they lie in the sun or lean on a stone wall & talk. Or sip Carta Blanca on dark cement & listen to the amplified sound of beach bands, the drip of water in water closets where piss stinks, hurl & rush of the sea these small boys rise from, selling shells, to the clink of glass, to the cries of children, restless, sliding from laps toward that breathing body of water, water laced with sun, water the palm trees lean & listen to, murmuring their own windy songs.

And straddling the seawall in the full light of it, having crossed the street & come out of shadow, out of the shadowy wet cement bars where they'd had a beer, lured out by the sellers of necklaces & the coconut man who's parked his truck, he with his sons hacking off great slices of coconut shard from the liquid-holding core he shakes, so the gringos can hear, in the sun, in the full sun, wipe their brows, laugh, a little drunk, & promenade, gringos & Mexican families, carousers & beach boys & quiet young couples full of the promise of children, while all the while the band plays on, one band after another strikes up in the tinroof bars across the way, facing the sand & themselves, this cacophony blares like the sun their eyes hide from, shy & casually curious, sometimes blatantly so, they eye each other

   (& the music, *is* music, despite its cacophony, or even because of, tempo, a beat she occasionally catches another foot tapping to, as the woman in heels who, drunk, enters the bar doing a three-step, swinging her hips, sexy & laughing at herself, as the music accompanies her & all of them, scores their moods, their shifting movements, & drowns out the tiny sound she imagines these shells would make, with their bright beads like rosaries. She fingers hers bought from the boy, two of them hustling between tables, who had followed them out to the seawall, whose eyes, busy with the light of actually selling (diez pesos, señora! diez! on-ly ten pesos, señora!) whose light had gone dead when she said, provocatively testing her new-found strength, ocho, eight—a disappointment clouding the day, a disillusion in her willingness to share with them the sun, their festival thereof, this cloud a set insistence, dim & private, no, diez & she had bought willingly, two of them, ashamed at the evidence of her own loss.

   And so these clouds cross, making patterns on the blue-jade, the green-gray sea, & wind rustles the heads of trees above them, as if this were the day, as if nothing, nothing lay beyond it, no year to unwind, or looking back these thousands of years, so carefully marked on stones, those wheels that simply turn at intersecting points, neither unwinding nor winding-up, but like the music, like the breakers breaking all along the edge in quick succession, no beginning no end—

except that one's life, what then? blood on the blood-coloured stone to mark that point?—like a hole a sinkhole in the day. Or the eyes of the man at the market in Mexico City. It was dark, getting off the bus they almost stepped on him lying on the sidewalk, face up, eyes open . . .

seeing, that is what they do for each other, to keep each other here in the music, in the blaring music that continues as the dance goes on,

as it must, the boys, crossing back to the bar again, busy with selling, the coconut man & his sons likewise, gringos posing with hacked coconuts by his truck to photograph themselves, here— they say *here*, as if in disbelief, it is so hot here, the sun, invisible stone, presses all of their skins. & here the orange vendor comes calling freshness, pushing the bike that pushes his cart, & the couples, dan-gling their feet on the sea wall that humps in a low wind, are solicitous of each other, as they have always been, big brothers, big sisters, about-to-be mothers & fathers—the parade goes on of half naked & fully clothed bodies & as she fingers the camera with its telephoto lens she wants to move into the street, through an eye that is an extension & even impertinent accessory to the act of her seeing, she wants, not to see but to be—him? impossible. The young man on the seawall knows she is aiming at him though she pretends to follow the wavering movement of the orange vendor, & she focuses, carefully, his dark glance which is both *for* her & *at* her, a not knowing he can't quite tear himself away from but continues to sit staring suspiciously from around & behind several intervening backs, the closest of which, so close despite their mutual silence, turns finally & says, you're snooping, that's what you like about that lens isn't it, that's what it allows you to do. & she says yes, laughing, almost joyously, yes, she wants to see, into them, into their hearts as if that might let her know them but he persists, half-joking, it's like looking into people's windows at night, you're spying. & now she feels (o is it the eagle clutching a human heart on a stone frieze?) she is sacrificing them to her own curiosity, is she, is she taking over what is theirs or trying to? He says people who don't know cameras think you're taking their soul, & that man knows, he is trying to defend himself against your gaze.

O, she says, o. & she feels like the boy whose eyes had gone dead, stricken from the busyness of her own enterprise. Defiantly she continues to peer through the camera, focusing, shifting as the people's movements shift, but now they are only elements of a visual image, they have closed down into visual integers, hermetic & hidden as perhaps, they have always been.

When he says he's going for a walk she comes with him, only they don't get far in the heat beating down around them. They stop at some steps, both of them instinctively drawn to the shade embodied there by a cluster of palms where two old men sit conversing, very much at their ease. She wants to take a picture of them but they're out of range &, focusing on a solitary fallen coconut resting ridged- or spiney-green against a sand that has lost its brilliance here but still lies soft & ready for imprint, any foot, any passing wind, she clicks the shutter knowing none of it will turn out, those patterns of shade & light, that cool soft sand & the hard solitary coconut plopped, dropped, onto it.

Invisibly she would turn & photograph him, even as he moves forward down the beach, familiar, so that she recognizes without seeing his step, volitional, quick, black hair tied back so nothing except the few wisps of gray that dart above his ears disturb his seeing, his very quickness moving him out of camera range & yet she knows him, knows he has no preconceived intent, only seeing as he moves onto the beach—*that* she can't picture, seeing him only in the telling to herself. & herself caught suddenly in her own viewfinder, establishing a view on what is so present to them they are *in* it—which is where she was & wants to be, she thinks, moving now, released, out of that marginal shade to the spot he has located.

Hot! he laughs, as she hands him the camera, & indeed this sand when they sit on it, in it, its broad expanse stretching unlimited down the coast, has the uncompromising brilliance of the street they descended into getting off the bus a few hours earlier, into Progreso, into a new year's day fishing town closed down for the holiday. They didn't know where they were or where the sea was, though it seemed to be to their right as they walked into a main street heading that way, it looked, into a gap at the end of open sky, open sea though they couldn't see it then, & in all that empty street, one man, a fisherman—They had gone to sit under a shelter, perhaps a bus shelter, some public shelter with a plaque she tried to read & this man ambled along & addressed them in Spanish, as if noticing they were lost, as if to give them directions which she couldn't understand. & Yo had said, well he wants to talk to us, & offered him a cigarette. They exchanged lights & the man sat down on the step with them. Yes he was a fisherman but today was a holiday etc. She pieced it together, but by bit, with the help of the dictionary & his repetitions. Big waves, big big waves, he showed them how big. But there were boatloads of fish out there. Where's the beach? That way. & further directions she couldn't understand. Is it good for swimming? He was giving advice, but what? Kept repeating that word, swindle, she knew it was swindle, having looked it up in the dictionary. He continued to talk but she gave up trying to follow him. He was drunk & companionable, wanted company, & now she heard the music coming from what must be a cantina across the street behind its anonymous corrugated iron. His friends would be in there drinking, & he had come out alone, had seen them, & wandered over, obviously wanting to talk, to Yo, the usual questions, ¿japonés? ¿japonés? Yoshio would nod & smile, he never spoke, not having bothered to learn the Spanish, he simply smiled & the other would continue to talk, pouring out his excitement or curiosity. In all that sunlit street, broad as any smalltown attempt at boulevard but bare of plants, only stone, only the occasional rattly bus making a turn into, roaring through & then disappearing again, no one, no one except themselves & this man talking—she saw, thought she saw, what it was that might appeal to him, their coming together at this odd point in the infinity of a street that continued, in all its implacable stone, without them—

No, that was her, that was here, that was the day, or is, where now they are sitting on the beach to which the man directed them as they said goodbye in the dry & dusty street they walked down, straight down towards that gap in the sky. A new house being constructed in the sand, vegetation & lizards, a palm they had seen from further back, waving now over thatched roofs, beach bar below them—they were high up, walking out onto a long pier that curved into the luminous distance of the Caribbean, blue or blue green when the light shone full, & patched with duller blue, ocean blue, not this extraordinary green lucency, as the clouds passed high up, as the wind blew. She reminds herself that they are here, in the distance they had seen, a few yards from where the breakers continue cresting & surfing in on themselves, salt water, & how salty she realized when she flung herself in, salt tingling all over, salt in her mouth, her hair, her eyes, in the millrace of churnedup sand, sun, froth, in the onslaught of moving walls of water she could dive through, & swim, rising & falling with this watery harrow that combed the bottom, a sharpness of salt, a water that wasn't soft but combed, flared, flashed in the sky & sand of its two poles.

Are you going in? she was full of it, she knew, standing there before him with the towel whose rubbing only intensified the salt she felt everywhere in her skin, so her hair stood on end with the static of it, if static it was, sun burning into, she imagined, uncountable tiny crystals of salt refracting, dancing, her body covered with flakes of light, like scales, fish scales, herself full of the salt, its strength, flashing there in the sun.

No, I'm quite happy where I am. Was it a smile, a not-smile, a look & she saw in that look her own reflection, his knowing of her there, flashing in all her salty strength, his knowing her flaunting of it. Humbled she lies down beside him, wondering what *he* sees, his stillness like the stone under them. & thinks again of the absurdity of her long skirt in all this heat, its edge dragging in the piss & wet of the cement barfloor, of how it served as tent so she could undress on the sand, because in her north American stridency she had been *determined* to go in. & she remembers the two old men sitting in the shade of the coconut palms, perfectly at ease, perfectly located in their own spot. On all that stretch of sand, she had chosen to undress in front of them, she had interrupted their beach. Or perhaps they had simply viewed her as part of the ongoing spectacle of the day that continues to stream around & past & through them, they being so stilly present here, like him . . .

Look at her, he says suddenly, she loves that water. At first there is only beach & its various people in their various awkward relations to it. All *that* she has seen before, is part of, they both are. And then she sees her, a small brown girl in wet huipil who dances, dances up & down the breakers' bounce, launches her body on the breakers' downward furl, combs with her hands their white combs, disappears & comes up, wet blouse clinging with all its gay embroidery to skin. From a distance she is only a speck on the thin line that fronts this coast stretching to infinity.

She's trying to teach herself to swim, he says, I've been watching her for almost an hour.

Has it been that long? the beach continues to stretch, as the promenade does, as the pier, under the sun which hardly seems to drop, westward, or southward, depending on where they sit, & yet, yes, it has moved, or surely there are fewer people on the beach, is it the hottest part of the day? is it the time when everyone who lives here knows to go indoors, into the shade? Except themselves & this girl who continues to dance in the froth, up & down, up & down, paced she sees now by an older sister, who watches from the sand as she works her way slowly up the beach, launching herself into the crest of each succeeding wave & flailing, but no, not flailing, it's not that she tries or doesn't try, or even dries herself for one moment in her dancing under the breakers' overhang that frames her head, that froths, surrounding, a melee of salt & sand & wind, & then withdraws, & then she rights herself, held by its rhythm to continue as it twists again & froths up over her face or trips her—staggering backwards into the full weight of it, she disappears (sister waits a little more alert), & reappears, laughing, wrings her huipil in a second's pause before the next, wipes her off her feet. These two, one dry, one wet, progress slowly up the beach in a silent rhythm neither one will speak, the sister watchful as the other lost, in the pounding of the sea, continues to listen, dance, ring with what, only, waves speak, or only windy palmleaves, only sun, in a great silent mica jet, speak brilliance, speak the pound of the sea she hears sounding all day in her ears . . . & when he says suddenly, says with the energy of connection, as if, as if *this* were what the day were for, that's something you could do you know, you could teach her to swim, she is surprised & can't reply, has no good reason why she cannot, as she cannot speak of what she dimly hears, this song there in the girl's dance, not to be broken, as the day, the sea, or later, as they walk slowly along the promenade in the afternoon, paced by the sun which is dropping now, past children & dogs, past stragglers of the earlier throng, past dowager houses that face an opening sky thin trees rattle their palmfronds in, listen, except to say listen, how each tree rattles its own peculiar song.

      & is checked when he says, as if in answer, you seem more yourself today than you have ever been, & contradicts, thinking of all that surrounds them that has entered in, no no, it's less, less. He laughs, yes, he says, that is the same.

      It is as if she is midwave, suddenly, one of those water walls, have crested & dissolved & she appears on the other side, so *this* is what it is, only to realize it is all, all water— boundaries dissolve, as their distinctions do, sand sea sky one great cycle in the dance they dance there within each other. sun & cloud. What can she say to him who has so deftly dissolved them? to touch & yet, they continue side by side, & different, & lost in their mutual seeing of all that is out there. Returning at the end of the day, what does she know of how it was for him?

      Was it the fisherman, was it the fish they had in the bar for supper facing the sea, was it the child dancing in the breakers, what was the day for him? She doesn't know

& she could ask but when she glances at him standing there beside her, wrapped away in the vague tiredness of his body, rapt in the sun & the music & the sea, or what is left now that resounds in both of their bodies standing in the lineup at the bus depot for tickets, she sees that he is busy watching the women, two rather stoutish women with children, teasing each other over ice creams, mothers & children teasing alike, amid nevertheless motherly wiped faces, swinging earrings, exclamations, waiting on tired feet, the patience, hovering, like a school of fish, she thinks, the same thought runs through each of them without being said. & she would be them or in the watching she is them, as he is them, as they have gone out of themselves to be with the others.

    & when the bus arrives they all clamber aboard, tired, happy, salty, sunburned, a little drunk, & they, they choose the seats behind the seats they are supposed to have (not knowing their tickets are numbered), & when the couple whose seat they have taken understand their ignorance, they gesture that's all right, & sit down in front, a young couple, the woman pregnant, the man silently present to her, they lean against each other, his head on her shoulder. & further down there stands another couple, he American, tall, blond, with suntanned hairy legs below cutoff jeans, loud voice talking about some incident with a friend, & she, Mexican college student?, leans against him, looks up, above her bright-coloured Mexican skirt, & supremely disregards the rest of the bus, encouraging, flirting, commenting, while he clings with his loud voice to her eyes.

    And so they leave Progreso, leave the sea, & skirting the edges of the inland marsh where a boy in a boat catches the last fish, where herons stand solitary & leaning toward the sun, where imaginary turtles dive, & caught up in the real & fictional people, caught in the possible stories of their lives, they travel south into the lingering light, wondering as unreadable signs flash past them if this is the last bus, not knowing for sure but conjecturing as they stop at each small wayside place, as people crowd on away from the growing night or drop off at junctions where no one seems to live, over the flatness closing in, this bushland vine entangled, or these maguey fields, they continue slowly inland, inwardly lit against that dark that makes the land recede, turned in on themselves & momently diverted by an altercation between the ticket-collector & two boys at the back, each of whom swears he thought the other was buying their tickets, the ticket-collector wearily bangs the side of the bus to make the driver wait while he ousts them into the dark of another wayside junction, barely seen, only railroad tracks & a crude shelter past which, as the bus stands there, a battered car, so loaded down with people that its rear bumper just clears the tracks, bumps over & roars past into the night, past . . . it is familiar, that car, she has seen that car before in a dream & knows who's in it, people, people of the earth who escaped her, she had dreamt that car—or that car in its movement had crossed her dream. Another unreadable sign, it roars off into the dark. Turning to tell him, she sees that the Mexican-American couple have worked their way down the aisle toward them, she leaning rather pitifully against him, complaining of stomach ache, & although she speaks in English, the young Mexican husband in front gets up & offers her his seat. The bus moves on, into the outskirts of Mérida, street lights so high up they scarcely illuminate the road, & this town like all Mexican towns, barely lit, its 40-watt bulbs sending out a dim glow from kitchens or front rooms. Now they are making residential stops & suddenly the Mexican girl leaps up & gets off, waving to her American friend as he calls, insistently, futilely through the window, see you tomorrow? & she, you're going the wrong way, walks off toward home.

Did you see that? Yes, he says wryly, well she's not going to give herself to some American tourist. You mean, that was just a day at the beach? Sure. But they seemed so intimate! He shrugs & looks at her, grinning.

And is it just then, staring out of the bus, she catches sight of the monument in the middle of the road, & as they wheel past its illuminated words carved into stone, grabs a notebook, writes down 'El Mayab (?) es la tierra misteriosa y antigua . . . in which? (what was it?) . . . todo hablar en el silencio.' She cannot check it, the stone has moved into the dark, into their own past, & the page has only caught these words, flying in from outside, which she offers up to him, translating, or mistranslating, 'El Mayab (something to do with the Mayans) is the earth . . . mysterious & ancient . . . in which (I think) . . . everything speaks in the silence.'

You saw that out there? He looks at her astonished, as she at him. A wild surmise. & sees it in his eyes. Silent, they sit together as the bus carries them into the heart of Mérida.

1 – NIGHT (MERIDA

Look the moon is up, she'd said it walking home across the zócalo where it hung between some leafy trees (unnamed) glossy in lamplight where the moths or insects flit. what is it? on the old benches, the old men. she jumped. they were sitting among them, on slats that dig into your backbone, not curved quite right, or missing green, green slats & ironwork arms, still one or two of the daytime men, taxi drivers & teenagers, still smoking, still joking, chatting, poking fun, as the night wound down. & look, he'd said, the shoeshine man's still up. old man, old shoeshine man who sat, infinitely still, head hung forward hands between his knees—he's not so old, has he fallen asleep? he sleeps here, old & indifferent. all night dark things wing over his head between the leaves. are they birds or bats? or flying beetles, knocking between the masses (indian laurel?) glossy like the night they can't quite see for lights, the moon, she said, the moon is up. something fell into her lap. what is it? a seed, a seed.

are you asleep?
no, just dreaming. no more dream than he is turning, sliding his arm under her neck as they fall toward each other in this impossible bed, yes impossible, i can't sleep, o the beds of Mexico with their dips & drops, think of it, all the people who've slept here (the skin of his body warm in itself, apart from hers, his skin, even in the night, even under the wind of the slowly turning fan, rises against her, solid as earth) city women who come in from shopping, children who lie here napping (through open doors, lightly ajar) the tourist & his lover (o here we are), his body turns from the dip of the bed to the ridge she lies on, rising, as she is falling the moon is rising, outside double doors so thin

in the wind, outside slatted doors that reach, like guards, half open, half awake, to the ceiling, fan works, slowly in the heat their two skins generate, heat of his arm around her on that bench the cool blew, & dark things fell out of the tree toward them. going home he'd said look at the moon, & it was white white in the dark. i thought of us walking, *home*, she said, isn't that funny? eyeing the upper portals light shines through (moon out there?) does it feel like home? (only the moon is bright & night empties the colour except where indian laurels shine, glossy & green by electric light their forms slump under, waiting for them all to go, waiting to cross the fence to the lawn where it says no walking) home? (turn on the light, yellow walls will show, spit-flecked or snot- or pencil-crossed. someone's been counting days, she'd said, las dias, someone had wanted to know how many, keeping track, & what do you do when you know? have we lost count of the suns, los diós, lost?) could you *make* it home? he persisted (home, this room? a shape they knew, even in the dark, knew how to find, though they couldn't remember the name of the street, or number, how many doors down from the corner, only by instinct knew, this doorway, in where the cars go, over the floor & past the soiled upholstery, past the desk, past piles of laundry & into, at back, their courtyard. yes there was something hidden about the way these buildings opened away from the street, flowering away, hidden away, at heart—)

                              but nobody knows where we are, she said. is that a condition of home? (heart in a kind of panic, no nobody really knew where they were & what if her child called out? there were roots, pulled them back through earth to people they knew, north, particularly north where the cold light of the stars sputtered & flared, that was home, where her child was & the trees, trees she recognized grew in the rain) but isn't that why we left, he was saying, to get away from all that. was it? to escape from roots & be lost for a while, hidden in the heart of a different & dry earth. but if you were *lost* (counting crosses on the wall, catching your eye on the moon as it wanders past these foreign trees, glossy in all their leafage dropping strange lost seeds on the people below) . . .

& you, she said, eyeing the doors, do you feel at home? keeping
her eye on the white track of the moon they hardly closed off, hours,
counting their sound now, one (coming in) . . . two . . . what is it?
three o'clock, three o'clock & all's well. isn't that what they used to
call? everything continues as it was, everybody go on sleeping (no i
want to be out with the moon that keeps wandering over town,
looking in everyone's back room) it all goes on, he was musing, doesn't
it? wherever we are. i suppose i feel as much at home here as anywhere—

but how can you say that? she thought aloud, & when she
lifted herself on her elbow in the grey light there was his face, just
visible, calm, the smiling line of jaw, hair black on the pillow, eyes
watching her. what do you see? your eyes are black & i can't see what
they say. perhaps they say nothing. lightly, lightly, he laughed up at
her—

& they were back in the park, in the zócalo under the leafy trees,
they were back on their bench, watching, discreetly, the solitary
shoeshine man slump into sleep, into absence, into a profound indifference to them all, his blue box not even blue in the night, tucked away
by his heel & utterly useless. he has no place to go, she said, he's
always on that bench whenever we come by, doesn't he have any
friends? o yes, others like him, except they have a place to go. do they
give him anything? sometimes they share a Pepsi.

as a little breeze got
up, they watched him cross his arms tighter around himself, pull his
jacket away from the slats of the bench, hawk a gob of spit, gaze up
blankeyed, doesn't know where he is, & slump again. that's as much a
place to be, he said. & she shivered, as the seed dropped like an insect
into her lap.

ISLA MUJERES

Water's deep sea (green/blue) caribbean: Puerto Juarez at the tip of the peninsula where the bus stops, bus shelter, not much more, hotel or two, a dock, a beach palm-fringed, this, this is a picture, here is the bluegreen they'd seen on paper, see now continues, this actual sun, this real woman on a boat approaching them where they now stand, by coconut palms, on the verge of a bluegreen sea extending luminous sky. & they get off the bus, they follow the others, hurriedly, to the dock, every two hours the launch they just get on, they get on with the baggage & other tourists, not making sure how much the ticket costs, only to be on & the boat roaring up to the start, throttle open leaving that dock & ladendown, cut deep into pure depth that billows, almost within fingers' reach it furrows, into that central & deep milky aqua zone, clear now of either shore, in the middle of a great expanse of sky & sea.

But even in the middle, even free, they are approaching, she can lean out over the gunnel & see it, the island, or isla, 's' sounded (like grease, crease), crinkled by palms in this sea it somehow, a thin wedge of land aflare with trees, simmers in, heat, in the infinite forward rush of water they cut backwards, streaming, yes, it is streaming *forward*, the sea, toward that horizon light open like a mouth—only a thin edge of island stops the water streaming as she looks, & as she looks, looks down: translucent, bubbles, spray, an upward arc of water forced by the weight of their own displacement into sun, flare/flash, in a flash they have gone & the fish are elsewhere.

& this continues, this swallowing of surface in depth,

or up again, outward, eye moving all around, & turning out toward the others, notes how they are all born inward to their own desire which flares up in their gaiety, each of them secretly expecting something of this place they are now approaching, she wonders, glancing at him what does he expect, who catches her quick glance & smiles. He is enjoying the boatride, he who doesn't like water, she can tell by the way he faces into the wind, jaunty, hanging by one hand to the roof. Beyond him & further inside, the figure of the woman she'd been sitting next to, dressed in white huipil with the worn rebozo of her class slung round her neck, baby sick, a runny nose, halfclosed eyes, dozing, loose in her arms, & she erect, alert in her curiosity about those others, those on the other side of the box she sits on, with as much right yes but not evidently, evidently she is invisible to them, this large family, many bags, the boy tired & tearful, his toy won't work, distracted by older sisters pointing, mira! mira a la isla! & then the other who had entered from the prow so young she couldn't have been more than seventeen, her boy-husband standing back, a little helpless, mother holding the baby who, hair petted in curls, in new clothes, was screaming (tch! tch! tch!), the grandmother smiling apologetic, no le gustan los barcos. She had got up so the grandmother could sit with the boy. Fondled & soothed by two pairs of hands, he gradually cried himself to sleep, the others leaning over, ay pobrecito, laughing, joking about this infant possessed already of discrimination, character, in short a personality.

      While the other, native to the island, continues to watch, as they all do, the fuss. Her own child, hearing the noise, had begun to whimper but soon calmed as she bent to it, & then glanced up, at the other pampered one, a look full of the recognition of how her own, quiet in her arms & sensible, could be nothing but, sensible, to a necessity she herself as they all do, bend to. & they continue to sit or stand composed as the island enlarges its white stones or pickets so that now they see hotels or something larger, some formal looking shape, ships, a navel base, they see cafes & boats, a sea wall. Isla Mujeres, Island of Women who stayed as the pirates came & went, who stay now as the tourists come, or cross with them to go to town but always return home, enislanded. & how does she feel, that woman? invaded? or does she watch as one watches gulls behaviour, part of the peculiar life of her terrain?

We are, she thinks, momentarily, migratory birds, strange plumage from somewhere up north, though they don't know that, always they are glancing at him, wondering chino? ¿japonés? His hand lies peculiarly vivid along the railing, second fingertip missing where he sliced it off by accident. Shyly almost she covers it with hers his turns to clasp, & he is glancing into her eyes that are always asking, what're you thinking? are you happy? as if it needed asking or indeed had any answer. & seeking to unask it says, this is what birds do, skimming water like this. He laughs, you'd like to be a bird? Imagine what it would be like to move in your element feeling all around you air currents or, if you were a fish, currents of water. I've never thought about it, the human is really our element I suppose, all the funny little currents on this boat—he gestures toward the people she has just been watching & the smile they exchange is complicit, a stretching out into eyes which break like the surface of water with recognition, each, at seeing what the other has seen. He says, in the eye of a camera nothing is foreign you know. Yes, she thinks, but doesn't say, I want it to be that way for me too, but it isn't.

Caught up in the crowd & climbing over the side of the boat & onto the island, they are in the midst of crowds, baggage, people who greet each other in a language they don't understand. Sand drifts softly over the pavement barefoot children dart from, around the seller of soft drinks, his vials of different coloured syrups leaning against the tray, as they, offering their few English phrases, seek to catch them: you want a boat? you want a room, señor? clean, good price. & the young northamericans in cutoffs disappear with their backpacks, with their copy of Mexico on $10 a day, & the circuit begins, in the heat, the confusion of names & streets, the momentary shelter of white vestibules, ¿hay un cuarto para dos? ¿cuánto?! while the others clustering in the street confer, this book's way off, well I'm sorry you guys, *last* year we could have got by on 5 bucks each.

The one they find is new, brilliant white in the sun, same price as all the others (island, island) but the boy who takes them up the outside staircase to the third & top storey, to a room that hangs out over the street— ¿señora? clean & shuttered from the light, looks pleased when she says es bueno. Outside on the balcony he calls to his brother sweeping the other one across a space of air, hokay!—they will bring up the register when they bring up the key. & at last they can lie, flat out, under the slowly revolving fan, cool water (not to drink), shuttered windows (expensive privacy), their own small balcony from which to view the passage of the street through its canyon of adobe walls toward that brilliant sea, sand, drawnup fishboats, shouts, a radio playing some-where from some walled compound they'd looked down on as they climbed the stairs, children, dogs yapping, laundry, someone hammer-ing: island shifts around them with the spinning of the fan, shifting currents of their own room cool their skin to the touch of clean linen she stretches into, feeling all of it, but o, it *is* expensive.

He, savouring his cigarette, abstracted, thinking perhaps of the boat or the people, of anything & nothing she can imagine, surfaces with the words, well it's not something we can afford, so let's enjoy it. Will you miss the other one? she wonders. O no. She thought of the wall behind their pillow & its crosses, shabby yellow walls, the tile floor, & their getting up each morning to the sounds of water as the cars outside were washed—*that* was luxury, those few liquid splashings in the heat of an otherwise stony courtyard, Oviedo, olvidado (forgotten), its decrepit spaciousness reduced to minimal furniture, bare walls, its very bareness somehow— But you liked it there (she searched for the words), somehow it fitted? Yes, in a funny way it did, I liked its unobtrusiveness.

Here everything clamours in the sun, the tourists with their brilliant costumes on, the tongues, all languages, even the young men, perhaps they are sailors on leave, she can hear them roaring up the street below on motorcycles which seem to zoom everywhere over the dirt & paved roads. & the young men who called out to them from their boats, fishing boats turned into tourist vessels, men tanned & medallioned who would take you fishing, take you to beaches, take you all around the shore. She wants to go out into the street & see this place, even if it *is* the hottest part of the day. She feels thirsty & takes out the bottle of tequila & the one remaining lime. Want some? He shakes his head, he is dozing off, but she likes the bitter taste of it with its varying redolence, like the earth she thinks, how does she know?, she has never eaten earth. She has swallowed sea, & the image of all that cool to slide their bodies into, its salt, even its bitterness, tantalizes. O don't be so impatient, he wants to sleep & why not? there's no hurry, & already she is cool from the fan, it's only the *idea* of swimming in that exotic sea, those colours—already you've forgotten the day out there, you've forgotten how hot your body was, how cool the water will be, & the sun the sun will not stand still, though the shutters make you believe it. O let's go out, she says, if we fall asleep the day will be gone. Let's find a beach, there's a good beach for swimming at the other end of the island, shall we look for it? He opens one eye & surveys her, with the faint outline of a caustic grin. On foot?

Why not? she is exhilarated, turning, turning like an invisible gull falling already into the street, the sun, the blue blue air. He has a better idea.

And not till after the confusions of getting it—¿cuántos pesos? ¿por una hora o el día? how many hours do we want it?—the two boys lounging against the wall or rearranging them in patterns, no one else was renting, & the father indifferent to all but the business-transaction—he wants our tourist cards, aquí! aquí!, he's going to show you how to run it—one of the boys with skilled nonchalance had kicked it into action, was twisting the bars with a flick of the wrist & rapidly indicating parts —any gas? ¿que? ¿hay gasolina? si. how mu . . . ¿cuánto? no sé. Pedro! si si, completamente, I think he says there's enough, do you know where the

brakes are? it was only then he'd said abruptly, I used to ride one. &
getting on she feels strange: her legs stick out awkwardly behind the
intense curve of his back, manifestly determined as he tries the gears.
They set off with a flying jerk that quickly stalls. He kicks it over
several times & they try again, this time taking the corner at a slithery
angle & as she looks back she can see the boys gazing after them, this
crazy couple, the skinny white woman & the middleaged Oriental
hunched fiercely over his machine.

They enter the main road & wobble
a little past the boats, past the stores & people on the street, hola!,
someone waves, no boat they have wheels, & the sidewalk flashes by as
they pick up speed, hitting the first of the speed bumps at the naval
base with a smack that lifts her off the seat & down to cling a little
tighter (this thing moves!), but at the next one he rears up the front
wheel (remembering how) & they streak out of town, now they are
going fast & the bike dips at the curves (gravel, she imagines skinned
flesh), now she no longer surveys the scene, gazing from their rapid
seat at small adobe houses, tavernas, a monkey in a dirt yard, at the
lagoon, at sudden bushes & vines that whip by almost within reach, or
butterflies poised in the suck of their passing, now she keeps her eyes
on the road, her knees gript tight, face tucked in behind his shoulder,
& he is bent on speed, she can feel the strength of it rushing through
his arm outstretched to the bike, he is riding high & she cowers a little
as they hit the next turn. Slow down a bit. We're not going very fast,
he calls back, & she thinks that is probably true, but the road keeps
unwinding faster than her eye expects—when a noise beats up behind
& passes with a roar, two young Mexicans on another Honda. See?
The road slows down & she begins to see again—bushes, a thatched
roof, the sea, moving in & out of focus. Slow enough to imagine how
he sees it—they are a moving movie lens—

End of the road, he calls—& she
catches a sign, PLAYA GARRAFON—as they turn to, now, a long
(slow down!) descent on gravel—something about (don't brake! he
does) 'pescados de colores'—slithering down to parked cars, other

bikes, on a steep decline to the bottom where he puts out a leg to stop
them going over, stop. they wheel it to a spot against some bushes,
walk to the edge, rocks, to a thatched-roof hut below them, big bright
sign, BEBA PEPSI, people sipping drinks, sitting (she is still weak-
kneed) & at their feet sea rushing on to sand, sea, an immense brilliant, risible & shining, splashing against the earth it seeks to reduce to
flecks of laughter.

   Cliffs, slopes, at various planes & heights, various
canyons they climb or slide down, protecting the camera, dragging the
bag with two Pepsis & a towel, down to that water, hiding, under its
broken surface, a not very weed-ridden coral reef. & clearly, by the way
the swimmers are spaced, those standing rather aimless in the shallows
splashing, those wading further converged in a crooked line & calling
to each other, those further out puffing through snorkels like small
whales, there is a channel one can swim through, sand at bottom, &
the going, if a boat passes & there are waves, can be rough. She is
eager, stripping already, thirsty for the water—you coming in? No, go
ahead. He has the camera out, is perched on a rock already perceiving
through the lens various individuals about him. She hesitates a moment, if they are here together then where do they meet? can she
expect him to meet her, openly, on her ground? but is that what this is?
He has his eye fixed to the aperture, he is up against his particular
opening—rock & people. And the water, which she stands in, up to
her ankles, feet shifting grains of crystal sand, swirls, likewise clear but
fluid & restless round her skin, round all of them, swimmers the sea
takes in a like embrace, a brilliance that makes her smile, makes her
forget, irresistibly caught in the orifice sand sun sky create, this smile,
this dazzle dances, pulling her in.

   Cool, cool up to kneepits, up to groin
& then—duck, dip, flings herself, into the full glide of water over belly,
shoulders, chin. & gazing, face down to the streaming clearness of it,
sees what they see, those others with their masks, their fins, o a quick
glance of colour, brilliant as birds, scarlet, yellow, & black bands as the
dimmer shapes of whole fish dart by, into the mass of coral looming

ahead. o the revelation of it, sea in all its massive swaying gives, currents, bodies, quick glimpses, maybe hundreds she thinks, all feeding in these brittle holes, these cavities. She wants to jump up & shout to him but when she looks back at the beach he has turned & is climbing up the rocky slabs with his camera, looking anonymous.

Now she is alone with sea, or underwater is, looking, for as long as she can stay, for these elusive colours which light up the reef—she can't quite see, or sees only dimly, eyeballs blurred by their element. & coming up for breath, is disappointed, coming up to sit on the roof of their world, this rock whose lacy forms jut surprisingly firm, & sharp, waves of water shifting her onto a jagged peak unless she hang on, in the lift & fall of it, like some mermaid, some other there too, across the way, likewise perched. Both of them exchange a smile as the men come up the sandy channel between them, blowing water, taking off their masks & huffing from out there where the sea moves, where she will swim in a moment, if she can give up this desire to see, see them down there under her feet, under the smiling surface of the day.

Boy it's great out there, one of the men says, removing his mask & shaking his head like a wet dog. Someone who speaks her language, assumed she spoke his. &, the ease of it, she does. Lots of fish? The little buggers'r everywhere. Beautiful colours? she asks, can you see them? & he responds, hey you ever used a mask? go on, try mine. you haven't seen anything yet. No, no, you gotta get it over your nose completely & breathe through your mouth. Like this, see? It's gotta be tight too so the water can't get in. She winces as he tightens her hair in the buckle but feels grateful: another opening in the day.

And now she slips into the channel— breathe through your mouth, he calls. At first the mask steams up with the force of her exhalation—come on, calm down, it's your element too. And she forces herself to let go of sky & fall into wave, into a swirl of water round the coral suddenly clear, & there, hand's reach, a school of tigerfish, turning & curving with the movement of water, skim sand below her, hover, one or two making forays to the coral then returning, &, as she strokes closer, spurt ahead, hover, as if waiting for her, spurt & then recover, equanimity. It's a slow underwater dance of follow the leader, she follows, through the channel & out to the deep end of the reef where coral forms huge mushroom-shaped clusters, canyons where anemones grow, strange underworld formations light fails to reach the bottom of. Here other fish, vivid as parrots, wave their colours, waver, weave through branching growths of coral & she follows, turning with them, twisting, tucking her legs up in a slow motion whirl in the reef holes where they lead her, turning themselves to look, pale eyed & curious as she, almost, touches . . . water. Always there is this streaming past her skin & theirs, always a movement slides between them, water, takes them in its own going never for a moment still, the whims of fish, her moving impulse, share it, swim within its streaming further & further, far, so when she surfaces again the beach seems to have drifted & her own eyes, dizzy with incessant movement, have lost their focus, shore, none of it familiar, simply sits at the water's edge. Until she spots the crimson & blue Pepsi sign flashing, tinny in the sun, & is aware, suddenly, of her own coldness, shivering: exhilaration run down has left her outside the reef & she is cold, tired. Time to go back, climb out, & feel the sun.

Water, water seems to drag at her feet as she swims, as she staggers, dizzy, up out to the world, to the man (thank you. how was it?) the black rubber strap almost part of her skin (tremendous) flicking drops that crystallize in the air, so transparent, so thin (any time. thank you.) to finally sink onto her towel its warm nap like fur rubbing her back into her body.

Yo isn't around, probably somewhere up on the rocks, probably hot if he didn't go in. She lies down, stretching as much of her as she can onto hot rock, feeling sun irradiate the inside of her eyelids, imagining bone & blood lit up. Why is she trembling? it was dark down there & she hadn't noticed, dark, & the cold fluid she swam in is still streaming through her body in an electrical charge she can't turn off: 'power of the sea'—o the dream, its power. She doesn't want to be anywhere but here, though she'd thought, yes she'd *thought* she had, in a curiosity that threatens to consume the world, simply sun & rock, a place to be. Sits up. The sun is definitely lower, where is he? Still trembling, she gathers up the towel & her clothes, climbs up over the rocks & spots him further up the slope, perched on the edge of a big slab ringed by bushes & small trees. He is sitting in their shade, smoking a cigarette & looking perfectly at ease.

As she climbs over their roots she sees that his boulder straddles a small crevice filled with bits of used paper, dry leaves, old butts. Whatcha doing? Getting out of the sun. (dry earth smells.) It's a shady little place all right, she almost shivers. Good for taking pictures. He gestures beyond the bushes. What're they doing? He shrugs. Take a look at them. As she looks again, their faces seem to rise & float above the bushes with the peculiar flatness of Mayan profiles, only their bare shoulders visible, & vulnerable, their heads float in the intense light of afternoon. They look like gods, she says, like faces on a stone frieze. Well whatever they are, he grins, I've taken several shots of them. (Of course.) And you? Fishes & men, she thinks, & as their eyes meet through the smell of dried leaves, smoky & sweaty, the skin of late afternoon, she reads, he offers it, his being there: simply alone & seeing, what is given.

2 – NIGHT (ISLA MUJERES

Well is it time to sleep? despite wind swirling in through their shutters, making pools & currents in the air they are lying in, the burning of his cigarette seems close at hand, his voice comes through the dark of the room fully awake. she wonders what he has been thinking, his voice so fills space between them, resonant as a bell—but that was the church whose bell they'd heard only walking back, its levels of sound tolling toward them as they retreated through the streets, not streets, roads, not roads but channels, rapid with laughter, with conversation at open doors, small children crying or playing, parents exchanging talk in dimlit rooms she wanted to look in, but always their sidelong glances, a slight hush in the talk as they passed, prevented her. glimpses, she thought, just glimpses of what it's like, this hidden life, bodies, within body, of land this island is, in the dark enveloping sea . . .

are you awake? yes yes (surprised at her own quickness, she had been drifting again), i was just thinking (how can she put it? & now that she's asked herself, what *has* she been thinking? what has he? no use to ask, he never likes to answer, or does—nothing, he'll say, & she won't believe it. her words hang in the air in the same way & she hadn't meant to hold him off). i was thinking here we are three storeys up in a brand new hotel, our own bathroom even, & down below us there are all those streets, all those dark adobe houses all that unknown life going on . . .

feel like a tourist eh? he laughs. she resists even the label, i hate being a tourist. so do i, he says, but that's what we are, especially here. you mean in this room? no, on this island.

but why? why on this island? (& even under the surprise in her question, instinctively resisting what she feels he is going to say, she hurries back, back to that original sense of it, of island (women), something about being on an island she wants to convey to him, the ease of those birds—what are they? she'd asked the waiter, gesturing—with long tails navigating the oncoming night. he'd smiled, politely, above the towel draped over his arm ¿las gaviotas, señora? (didn't she know!)—but they weren't, as she looked it up in the dictionary, anything like the gulls she knew, they hung in the air there, perfectly at home in all that restless space (rising like owls, who soar through the night, who escort her to that place, horizon, she escapes (the dark she had known, they return to)

       because it's an island, he is saying, once you're here there's nowhere else to go, it's a setup for tourists, look at that big hotel we passed (signs on the beach 'reserved for guests,' 'forbidden beyond this point,' something like that. they were walking down the beach, they were going to walk all around the shore—) but people still live here, still fish, you just have to walk the streets to see them. yes that's part of its appeal, isn't it? that's how they hook people like us, a glimpse of native life for us to gawk at, & don't we gawk! the ultimate tourists. but how could we not be? she asks defensively. sure, that's our role. he was butting his cigarette & she could almost hear the shrug in his voice, as if the issue were closed, a wall, a wall she didn't see, what was she resisting?

       in their walk they were going to walk all around the shore, they got as far as the nightclub they hadn't expected, low & white under the trees, no sound, no music coming out, no cars, except for one elegant ford parked silently by the open door. it was the trees & moon out there—wherever moon is they are, on the surface of earth, they have their dreams but moon, moon keeps wandering everyplace. & the trees remind her of the square, of the night they had sat there & he had said, look the shoeshine man's still up. is he right & the island, somehow in its streaming, makes them forget: the square, the night, one shoeshineman who continues to sit there—

when i was in San
Miguel i spent nine months on the public square, he is saying, every
day i sat on the same bench, just sitting until i was part of it. she saw
him sitting, she saw the old men & shoeshine boys, the orange vendor,
each in their appointed places, each carrying on their subtle & silent
conversation—but that isn't her way, she is running back to this island
in the dark of the sea, to the sea running yes to a limitless horizon,
nonetheless she asks (does she want to hear?) & what happened when
you became part of it? (not quite believing) nothing 'happened,' except
that i was no longer outside it. (of course, & isn't that what she—?)
& that's why you like the zócalo in Mérida, but even here you know
you can feel it in the wind & sea, in the way the whole island moves.
but that isn't what he feels, i'm not as romantic as you, nor as
young, he underlines it, the square is just about my speed (i can't
drive, he said as they both stared down the road ahead that glimmered
in the dusk—

     & she won't let them harden onto separate benches (we
have to get out of here, she said) & in despair reaches toward him, her
hand encountering his shoulder's bony firmness in the dark, persisting:
are we really as different as that? you love water, he laughs shortly, i
like earth, isn't that what our signs say? it's true, she had told him that,
but she didn't want to play with their signs, she didn't want to play. no,
i mean really? (i mean, let's go, it's getting dark—the colours of the
earth, the four quarters, stretching away to an impossible horizon.) she
could hear him smile, or was his breath a sigh, as he rubbed his hand
thru her hair, it doesn't matter does it?

     & lying beside him, her anger
ebbing away, she could imagine the dark as an element that surrounds
them, something, like fish, they encounter each other in, as water
washes around the island & even in this room they lie not in each
other's arms but in an element their arms move through, to touch each
other—even as she reaches up to kiss him as he reaches down, & their
mouths meet, even as his tongue enters hers & rubs its wetness against
her own, she remembers suddenly what it is, she remembers, not the

wall as they turn the corner, not the white building that says 'water board, water, potable' (cisterns? wells?) not the arch & gate as he walks on, but the cemetery she saw glimmering, low buildings like round heads or native houses rising out of the dark, & the words as she ran to catch up with him, do you know what's there? (his tongue is rubbing, even now, away away from her own) a village of the dead, existing there, beyond the wall.

UXMAL

¿Dónde está el bano de las damas? taking the secondclass bus to Uxmal & having to use the secondclass waiting room, where the washroom's locked, or what she thinks is, name fallen off the door. & he points, just points, with a supreme indifference. Does she say it then so awkwardly? or does he know that when he speaks her eyes will go blank, panic, she has forgotten every Spanish word she ever knew. But he points to the door which is the one she tried, & she says no, & someone else explains it's closed, cerrado, o & she was right it wasn't just a broom closet but where can she go? & they tell her to go round & over into the firstclass waiting room—official sanction then? But the bus is ready to leave & has he climbed aboard, the driver she last saw leaning against his vehicle with those other casual & confident stars of the depot? When he climbs aboard the show's begun & waits for no insignificant passenger in the washroom, who will not be missed (except by Yo, & he can't speak Spanish). It's a three-hour busride, even if she can't shit yet—well, that's the actual reason, isn't it, hoping the large jugo de naranja would do it, no more coffee no, racing back through the waiting room, past the guard (don't stop me), & into the potent smell of piss & shit (an air, phew), plastic buckets beside each stool filled with stained bits of paper, everyone's variety: newspaper, toilet paper hoarded in purses, pages torn from magazines, extravagant Kleenex, & the stinking remains of individual bodies passing through in time—she is too pressured by. & tries to remember the seller of hot tamales squatting outside the depot doors, already, early morning, on spitstained, littered, & no doubt pissedon cement (is that where they go? who live on the street in the public wind & sun) their day all day before them, children threading dribbled mazes in the empty fountain. 'You have to have a ticket to use this washroom.' (Where *do* they go?) But its no good, she can't imagine herself bodily into that woman squatting on the step, she can't imagine her day, its ease (or un-ease), as she walks back to the bus, wondering now where does it go, all that water & its contents, into what septic tank that doesn't process toilet paper?

Yo too is tense, same problem—any luck? no—as the bus driver swings into his seat with manifest definition, his partner nods, the door swings shut & they back out into the yard. This is the first bus they've taken with no shrine above the windshield, but he's very good, their driver, manoeuvering the long body of his vehicle at just the right angle to make those narrow turns, diagonal, honking their way through stone streets & out into the main road, into highway, sun (streaming everywhere), & fleetly past the Pepsi bottling plants, the airport maintenance sheds. Travelling west or south? The map, a little one in the guidebook, shows only the road threading page top to page bottom, marked with a pyramid, Uxmal, pirámide: it surprised her, that word, made it sound more esoteric than the terrain they were passing through could possibly lead to—possibly? pirámide: outcome. & where are they? She looks for the sun past his arm that stretches up to the baggage rack, braced against the movement of the bus. Discomfort: a falling apart. What can she tell him? to relax? that the body will look after itself, that she's long since given up trying to control its vagaries (has she? racing through the waiting room) & moreover how does she know what his must feel like, to him, what its importunities might be?

At any rate, the maguey fields keep rolling by, whole fields dry, & even the maguey dusty looking in the heat—'all of it one living rock (living?) . . . has wonderfully little earth,' this shelf, 'limestones risen from the sea.' & she could tell him that too but it is also unnecessary. Morning, no breakfast, & the coming awake a difficult entry into the world, each at their own pace. Their bodies in fact are here together, in this continuing suspension of them all in swaying space. Light streams in from their side (which means, south? she'll never get it straight, each time they turn, land turns) onto their hands, his arm, & there is nothing to do but continue, like the morning, to some unknown place.

But the moment she sees them she sees Yo has been watching all along, they are so vividly present: he whitehaired & erect, in his seventies maybe, she with a long grey braid down her back, stiller in her expansive flesh. They sit two rows up & across the aisle, as if they were attending some extraordinary event. Now he leans over to question a woman opposite about Campeche—that is the only word she catches, Campeche. Yes, the woman smiles, adds something, ah, he leans back & so informs his wife who nods of course, they had boarded the bus that said Campeche, hadn't they? You make sure you are on the right bus, that's all, but even the name, even the way he says it, 'Campeche,' disbeliev-ing, & the fierce attention of his back, suggest he knows this bus, suspiciously like any other, is taking them away. Now he explains & she listening, it is the way she is listening, not looking at him: he must explain, although she already understands, & the skin of her face finely lined, one bloodshot eye, turns *to* him, with sudden piercing assent, then away, soft wrinkled cheek again, a listening ear.

Marriage, she gestures at them, marriage is really a buddy system. Buddy? His eyes are caught by the women climbing on, baskets & children. It's what they use at children's camp when you go swimming, you always go out with a buddy, someone who keeps track of you—that way you can't disap-pear without anyone knowing.

He looks at her & she wonders what she said. Not the buddy system, perhaps, but the world, a swallowing. One mis-step & into . . . I mean—(to him they may look quite otherwise)— I mean, if one of us disappeared no one else would mind, we're only passing faces. We're passing faces all the time, he quips, & aren't they remarkable? That isn't what she meant, as he knows, & she knows he is choosing not to respond so that what she meant fades under the sun lying on their arms, the camera lying on his lap, & in his eyes, these women & children: yes, she thinks, as she looks, their flower-embroidered (hui-huipils, even the sound, weeps like a small bird) flesh, blooming giggles & quick smiles—one, a child, sending curious glances at them from around a sheltering thigh, to whom she decides to smile & who, before she turns to hide her face, suddenly opens, blackeyed, woman-to-be already figured in that luminous look.

After Muna's thronged plaza where the women descend, the bus chokes a little as it leaves the houses, gearing down for the hills, Puuc. Staring at the map, trying to see hills on it, or read those alien names—Xtepen, Yaxopoil—is it Uksmal? Ukhmal? Ushmal? ('thrice-built,' how can she know that & not know how to speak it?) she might have missed the first sight had he not nudged her, look over there. From a mass of treetops it heaves up out of the terrain, dark in places, stone, yet manmade, wrought, & that, rising above the thorny trees, is what impresses her most, its old familiarity.

A European girl in shorts hoists her pack as the bus pauses, others rise, this must be it he says, stepping down into the full meridian of sun, exhaust fumes as the long body of the bus, o she forgot to catch their faces, slides past, taking the old couple with it.

They follow other tourists up the trail to a gate, a government sign, various do's & don'ts in Spanish & English. While the ticket seller waits patiently for the right combination of pesos, a water tower on top of a house labelled 'reconstruction crew' leaks continuously down one wall—no one's home or they've laid off for the tourist season. Hot, hot, as the lingering touch of morning gives way to the weight of noon—& going without breakfast doesn't help, he says, eyeing the shacks with Pepsi coolers, guidebooks under glass, i've got to get something to eat. It looms behind them, that mass of stone they haven't yet confronted, even as she is caught by his 'got to'—how're you feeling? seeing him suddenly dwarfed by it, herself too, you all right? his grim, fine, i'll get two Pepsis, resisting the way it towers up into the blue, above them.

So that, sipping Pepsis, sitting on the rocks that ring, parklike in the dust, some tree, she feels herself back off, even as they face it. Even from here, from the cigarettes & Pepsi taste, people standing or walking (all those stones), even from the vantage point of paying patrons to a long dead show, it rises peculiarly human (what's inside? some child asks. rubble fill. what's rubble? stone rubbish. is that all?) The guidebook says there are five temples, three of them buried inside, three levels, five successive houses of divinity—but what—'superimposed' the book says, facades, masks, frieze, inclined slopes—led to the building of this off-oval, two-layer mound, smooth & round as some child's sand castle, incredibly heaped to the sun?

It's called the Pyramid of the Magician, she says, as they watch two Mexican boys start climbing, hauling themselves up its safety chain like humpbacked dwarfs (& how did they get the stones up? she imagines an enfilade of miniatures all toiling up its steep face, the cost of religion someone had said). According to the legend he was a dwarf (& why is she caught by that?) Aren't dwarfs always magicians? Yo asks, setting the empty Pepsi down against a rock, his voice seeming to come from far off, disinterested, just as one of the boys starts to run, side to side in zigzag motion, that ends suddenly as he disappears into a cavity halfway up.

It's such a strange story, she persists, ignoring his attempt to confound dwarfs & magicians. But there is something about the day that gets in the way of their speaking to each other. It begins with a dwarf whose mother was a witch & hatched him out of an egg (so far back in time it can't even be told with any probity). She sent him off to challenge the king & the king said build a palace overnight or I'll kill you. His mother helped of course with magic (impossible, faced with the actual mass of stone where the second boy, still clinging to the chain, is looking around for his friend who emerges, beckoning to him, & they both disappear). So the next test the king demanded was one of endurance, that they should each drop very hard nuts on their heads, the dwarf of course to go first. The witch made a magic plate for the dwarf so he survived but

when the king tried it he split open his skull. So the dwarf
got to be king of Uxmal & she went off to live with a serpent in a
waterhole.

Well, so *she* was the magician, he said, looking through his
camera at the pyramid. (Was she? was that why they called the sculp-
ture they took from the first temple Queen of Uxmal, even though it
showed a man's head emerging from the jaws of a snake?) But it was
the men who had all the power, it was the men who were priests here,
& kings, & warriors. They wouldn't name the pyramid after a woman.
Why not?

They didn't even have a goddess creator & destroyer, she was
going to say, but when she looked at him his face was closed & unreadable, bent to the camera on which he was changing the lens, & she
realized it wasn't information got from books she felt he was challeng-
ing but her sense of reality. Besides, these were Spanish names they
were arguing over, these buildings long abandoned, their original
names lost in the trees that had grown up all around & through them
by the time they were found. & she suddenly thought: we will miss it,
caught up in our heads, in our cameras & guidebooks, we will miss
what we came for. I'm going to climb it. Go ahead.

& so, flinging
herself into the climbing, hands to the chain, feet to the steps—
awkward, too steep & shallow to walk up erect, not stairs but steps, not
made for walking, for what then ?—she straightens up halfway &
enters the cave. At once a darkness surrounds her, visceral in its smell
of dank stone turned inwards from the day, unlit for centuries, & the
very present odour of human piss, of well-used secret places, as if she
has entered the bodily cavity of some huge stone being. She feels a
panic, a feeling of suffocation in the unreadable dark, & remembers the
guide book had said 'you will need a flashlight.' So much for the
hidden temple then. Continuing up the safety chain outside in the
glaring light, she wonders what it is that pulls her toward a dark she
can't read or (since the chain is set so low it's useless, & she straightens, holding her breath, a little nervous, fearing to look back at the

steep ascent, & down, into all that shining space he sits at the bottom of, legs crossed under the shade of a tree, perhaps watching her, more likely picturing all their movements, these small figures crawling up the oval stone body of this giant, its contours surely female)—is it the disparity of act & legend, the slow historical process of this place built stage by stage by men toiling in the light of day—& the legend of its creation overnight by a woman, out of a spell?

Almost at the top, open to the sky, she hears the guard's whistle, shouts, 'bájo, bájo,' directed at whom? Norteamericano, barefoot in cutoffs, climbing over what's left of the roof. He's telling you to get down, someone calls. Why? You're not supposed to climb on the roof, didn't you see the sign? I don't read signs that aren't in English. Heady with his own elevation, there at the top, one young man standing on a mass of stone, dwarfed by it. But reaching the top after his sullen descent, she understands: close to the sun, at its zenith, noon, anyone standing here, as one could not on the way up (steps, steps of the sun?) stands aloft over a world that stretches all around, north, south, east, trees they were sitting under all pelt & growth of rolling bush that hides this limestone shelf, hills, risen from the bottom of the sea, sea itself only infinite borders of consciousness at those corners earth folds into sky.

It's silent on the roof of the world. Its steepness impels her to give up clinging to an earth that lies far below, to jump off, into the light & wind, the very heart of space—she recognizes as falling, as earth calling her back to itself—& shrinking, edges around a broken wall to the western face of the pyramid.

There before her lies the full extent of Uxmal, its white-rose stone gleaming in a quadrilateral grace lifting stained friezes in walls, in combs, an undulation of planes & dark heights crowned with trees, jungle she'd heard it called, that makes the place itself a transformation of earth. Climbing over serpent heads (one to sit on, like a throne) or down high steps, she turns to look up at the ornate face of the temple, its doorway, someone posing stands, just inside a mouth, heavily incised

eyes above a jutting nose. The camera, she thinks, would catch that
mouth, that man standing in front of its darkness there, but the face so
huge, how far down would she have to step to get it all?

Wait, one of a
pair of girls appears above the step below, I can't believe how steep
these stairs are. Both rise into view, in jeans, walking shoes, nylon
packs on their backs, to sink down onto the top step with a smile at
her, the smile of outsiders who recognize their shared alieness. She
could almost be sure, you're Canadian?, but only asks, where are you
from? Calgary, we took the train down from Palenque—had a great
trip. They've traipsed all through the site, without a guidebook,
fascinated, even to the crumbled ruin on the far hill. Prairie girls.
Anything worth going over for? Well, there are caves. Caves? Yes,
caves in the ground, you know—(she feels a drop, a slight tremor),
it's a fantastic place really—do you know what these masks are all
about? Does anyone, she thinks, except for their surface, faces
to climb, sand castles in the wild. They're faces of Chac, she names
him, the rain god.

And continuing her descent, wonders, *under* the
name? dry land, no water anywhere, but caves, caves. Somehow the
witch persists, chaotic mother, though all the images are male, Chacs,
Bacabs at the four corners, all ordered under the sun, all countable.

She
sees him threading his way between carved & toppled stones ahead,
faces, remnant of the pyramid & its surrounding temples. He has been
taking pictures, she can tell by the way he walks, lightly, as if prepared
to be caught, eye caught, stopt. She hurries to catch up, his shoulder
blades under the white t-shirt a radiant thinness in the heat she would
put her arm around. Yo. Yoshio. He turns, how was it? I met two
Calgary girls, she laughs, jubilant now, they said there were caves. You
climbed to the top of a pyramid to find out about caves? She grins,
abashed, where else? He points to a line of people in the distance
toiling toward some building (palace? so the Spanish says), &, as they
watch white calves flash in the sun as knee after knee under leder

hosen lifts over the same stone, it'd make a fine movie, he admires, Seeing the Ruins. That's not seeing the ruins. Too quick, wanting it to be something else, always. He glances at her, she had missed the humour, & then at the sun directly above them now—the day is getting on— & moves, while she, pursuing that image of a cave (what is it about stone?) fights off what is everywhere present, when that is all that is required, assuming his steps on the narrow trail through rock: only to follow the trail their steps unwind,

only to see how these buildings they have gained front each other across a courtyard grass withers, under the heat, a string of tourists passing through, colours like brief flowers, & everyone's eyes on the dazzle of incised line against the light.

An exhilaration, this stone, these great dark doorways whose lintels, like steps of the pyramid, must be climbed—a hand up, a hoist. He stations himself for a good perspective on the corner building with its columns & serpents, & she steps inside, into a strangely shallow room. It rises upward like a vault, no windows, only this massive stone exuding damp & mould in a downward displacement, through air, of its own weight, wrought, against itself, into this arching slope. She tries the next, & the next, all of them alike, all vaults, all windowless, & as he enters, asks, what could they have been for? no one could live here.

Already, seeing him come in from the day, his white shirt bright against his face that is always darker, eyes full of the shine of lens & light, she sees the polychrome image he presents, vivid. He glances around then throws out, burial chamber? The door's too big. She's seeing him framed there, one hand cradling his camera (what he will *make* of it), the other in a back pocket twists his body, single & resistant in the doorway there, the better to see. Man, she thinks, men with their distancing eye. She feels a pang of envy for that clarity, & leaning forward, you're standing in the light you know, bites his ear. As his hands disengage themselves to enclose her, she sees over his shoulder the grassy courtyard their cave looks out on & the small figures of all the others. So you've found a use for it (his teasing tries to meet her), & in The Nunnery too. She wants to say they didn't have nuns, but doesn't. His body feels warm & resilient against her skin already chill from the mould. Do you think these rooms were here for their doorways? she murmurs into his neck. Are we in one? he asks, withdrawing, & she thinks he feels framed. I'm trying to seduce you. You're playing with the idea of being a nun. But there weren't nuns here! Nevertheless—he grins, you're irrevocably christian.

Astonished, she walks out into the light & follows him down the steps into the heart of the quandrangle. Is she trying to read these stones with christian eyes? what does she or he or anyone take from them? Except a profound sense of order, of an order that once made sense, wholly sufficient to itself, the coming & going of sun & moon & venus tracked with human eyes & plotted in immense recognitions— forgotten now, or somehow mutely present? Do you want to use the camera, he asks, offering her what he is here for. No, she waves the guidebook, I'll stick with this.

Having walked through the ballcourt whose walls have left only grassy inclines & broken rings ('cannot be interpreted properly'), held up by two elderly ladies of a party stumbling up the tumbled bank of a massive ruin ('although badly destroyed . . . the remains prove that'), they divert to follow a path through grasses & thorn bushes to a tessellated structure called The Dovecote. It towers above them, lacy stonework crest of square holes sun plays through, all of it leaning crazily toward them out of the blue. Having drained his visual curiosity, he lays the camera aside & lies down in the grass. Aren't you going to walk through that arch? vaulted like the rooms below, but leading onto bush, a genuine passageway. No, I've had enough. I'm just going to see where it goes. He nods.

When she turns, having walked through, she turns, she has come through to the other side of the site, these broken open vaults exposed to sky, it is onesided this Casa de Palomas (where are the birds?) it is a false front filled with holes & she has walked through into what lies behind the scene, *escena*, sheltered place. What lies behind the scene is bush, a jungle of trees, grasses, cactus, none she can name, a thicket the small path finds its way amid, into a dip, hollow, & then, towards the sky, she lifts her eyes, another hill, all stoney, oddly treed, no hill, a mound. And suddenly she is in the midst of an immense plaza, for there, surrounding her rise ridges that are not ridges, trees grown out of fallen buildings, an ancient square, contrived & once inhabited, lost now, given up to hidden urges of nature, growth sprouting everywhere. They who knew the steps of the sun & moon, the steps of the year, who knew how to count backwards a hundred thousand years—did they who knew the beginnings, know this?

No one else around, & the path leads into a hollow, into the depths of day, heat, the stirring of foreign leaves on foreign trees, a conspiracy of insects. She is afraid but the path says come on. One is a visible number & she feels very visible walking down the path, she shuffles her feet, she makes a noise for the snakes to hear, so they can get out of her way—although she knows it isn't her way but theirs. The ruin, in all its monumental silence, says nothing to her, only stands, stands at the edge of an earth she descends, she chooses, between two paths, she keeps her eye on the mound as best she can, through the increasing foliage. And then as the path turns at the bottom of the hollow, across & to one side she sees a hole. Powdery white limestone opens on the dark, mouth—enough room for one person to slip into, lowering herself down.

She thinks of the Calgary girls. She remembers their enthusiasm, imagines a flashlight, rope. She thinks of limestone, of how it's given to crack, of how it sinks. She thinks of snakes. She thinks of the men who were priests, & the dark intensifies, a hole that recedes into earth pulling her with it, sun swallowed up by night where those underground mock those who would come, aha you have stepped out of place, you have stepped out of time, you will lose your face . . .

No, that is another story having to do with men who are gods.

Her feet are on the path & the ruin lies ahead but she no longer wants
to go there. The end of the story, she thinks, I didn't tell him how
the witch exchanges water for children she feeds to the serpent.
That is a sacrifice she can't understand & struggles away from. Perhaps
he is right, she wants her individual soul—'irrevocably christian' after
all.

She hurries back—feet send little stones skittering down the
ascent, little puffs of dust—she reaches the crest, the arch & through:
he is still there, both hands curled under his cheek, knees drawn up,
lying old & foetal like a dwarf fallen freshly asleep on the skin of the
earth.

3 – NIGHT (MERIDA

'In the middle of the town of tihoo' in a kind of ache . . . stop talking, branches, bones . . . 'in the middle of'—it keeps on talking, 'is the cathedral' . . . stuck in a tree, stuck between two branches, given a space too small, too small . . . 'the fiery house, the mountainous house, the dark house' . . . something is dropping 'in the middle of the town of tihoo' where it is dark, a skull keeps talking, keeps on dropping, spit

'climb back up to earth then'

what? wakes up, jumps up, what? sitting up. whatsa matter? mumbles. can't sleep. mmmm. turns over. deep, wherever he is, & she, stuck with the night, continues. where was i? someone said something about a town, Tihoo, town that continues, under the town of Mérida, under, cover of night, bones complain at the angle of her hips, on the ridge of the bed where the dip falls in, where he is lying, apparently at ease in sleep, in the dark of, it all continues, this jumble, bones in a tree & hell, is the square, 'in the middle of,' there is the cathedral—

:RUN, run, she wants to, fling up, break up, out of that earth, out of cramped bones & into, whatever lies out there, where open streets go, silent under the moon. but the moon itself—where would she go? no one there but the blue, shoeshine man sitting under the trees . . . hell is having to be here, she thinks, suddenly seeing him, feet sunk into earth, even trussedup in the old shoes by the blue box, jittering, constant, into the dark he can hardly bear to move, his feet the only movement in a square which the dark cathedral mounts, closed, & utterly still. hell is this constraint—

she must get up, move, even to, piss, might as well. tile at least feels
cool underfoot & using moonlight filtering through the high lattice-
work door, she enters the bathroom, dense, black, but by feel or by a
kind of instinct, walls are walls & solid after all, finds the toilet &
sitting feels warm piss drain out of her, drain tension out of her hips,
trickling into a water she only knows is there by sound, & disappear.

he
is awake too, or halfawake, & the bounce of the mattress when she gets
back on lifts him, silent but conscious? she can't tell, can't tell how
wide awake he is, to make a like trip. burying her face in the sheet she
listens to the trickle he makes behind the partition at her head, a long
& apparently endless dissipation. & nuzzling her face deeper smells the
sheet, it smells thin, or is thin, smells of cotton worn thin by people's
sweat & come, the people themselves long gone—but something stays,
what then? an image of faces pale in the darkening air, between sunset
& moonrise a crack in the day self grows lost in—as he perhaps, lost in
the act of pissing, an action self disappears within, unconscious of her
listening, & turning deep within himself to that absence sleep is, he
gropes his way in the dark toward her. as he negotiates the foot of the
bed, she asks, how're you doing? (too bright, too wide awake) hot, he
mutters, tumbling in to lie face down one arm out to the floor. she's
sitting up. we're like two seeds rattling in a box. silence. the smooth
expanse of his back offers itself to her hand, but she thinks not to,
thinks she should get up & remake the bed, begin at the beginning,
thinks to do something complete instead of sitting in this half state,
half waiting, for what? there is only sleep to wait up for—

she says, the
shoeshine man's probably awake too (not even any moon out, just a
cramp in the neck) & then hearing the absurdity of it, a conversation
at three, four in the morning? she snuggles down behind & stroking
him repeats the line, halfsmiling, you can be in my dream if i can be in
yours.

mmm, he's turning over onto his side in the way he likes to fall into sleep & his voice comes out low & mumbly but definite, the shoeshine man's busy dreaming himself. she knows what he intends— you too, likewise—but does he know what the words imply, in that one dreamily decisive comment, you mean, we only *dream* ourselves? & she is frightened because it is there, the absence she wants to stay this side of, but how does he know? & how can it be?

the shoeshine man exists for them too. but has she ever seen his face? except in the downward plane of it, the downward cast of his forehead which doesn't even change when the others come up, the other who came up, who had a name, obviously, knew all about names & must have addressed him by his though she didn't catch it. who came walking definitively & directly across the square in shiny black shoes & white sports shirt, past the benches, through the orange peels & cigarette butts & dried leaves drifted around the one who had not moved, for hours, for days perhaps, walked straight up to him & delivered an immense tirade that was never answered, never even acknowledged—that worn body con- fronted perhaps by merely another phantasm of the day. what is he saying? telling him to shape up probably. & kicking his box, this citizen left in a rage while the body of the shoeshine man pulled the jacket around itself, crossed its arms & continued living.

he must be hooked on something, she'd protested, he's too out of it, he's stoned. no, he said, he doesn't have enough money for that, doesn't even care, he's just ... in the silence she'd said it, letting himself go—

CHICHEN-ITZA

The first thing about the day had been, unexpectedly, its cloudiness, a cool they woke to reluctantly, curled up against each other under a thin sheet, asleep, profoundly unaware that morning, this time, had crept in on them, not blaring & active, bicycles & cars already crowding the street, but wind, in a sort of absence, had lifted the imminence of noon, & in that cool space everything seemed to expand—women stared out of windows, doors left ajar, & in the plaza where the gardener was watering hibiscus, wind carried his spray fresh & even against their skin as they passed. Noon today would be an easy thing.

Good, he was saying, he who had not even been sure he would come, it's a great day for seeing the ruins. No doubt he meant the light which, now they are in the bus & passing, field after field, keeps changing, turning, luminous or shady—how it will not be glaring off the stone & into his camera lens. Still, she misses the ferocity of its presence, something to resist, heat, flat on their skin, theirs & everyone's, though she knows it bleaches vision—a kind of animal-presence everything struggles with, it fills space with a density she recognizes. Now, through tinted glass, green looks more green, but distant, & peculiar hollows the bus keeps passing—small dugout quarries? gravel for the road they are streaking down? (glad I'm not driving, he'd said) whiter, holes in the limestone shelf they ride the back of, high up & disinterested. This time they are heading south (no, east) anyhow sun no longer dominates these clouds, in all their eccentricity risen, brilliant & rapid, & moving with them, or away from, everything moving. She prefers to look out the window, to tease her eyes with that streaming, greenish, land, run swiftly beside them because, inside, inanity blurs the air like cloud or fog they stick their heads in.

This is definitely a first class bus, this is definitely a tourist excursion, but who the others are she can't make out. They have seats with a group of Americans, mostly middleaged men—one of them has a briefcase & a silent, possibly ten-year old daughter—but what are they there for, since obviously they are there for something, strenuously intent on observation: ya see that, Ed, no windows in those huts, just doorways. sure, easier to build em that way. dirt floors too—makes sense, huh? their women sure look clean though, look at em at that well. boy they could use a coupla good old Kansas windmills. Don't tell me you're from Kansas! a woman behind them leans across the aisle, for goodness sake, what part of Kansas are you from? Not that these clouds were moving with them—she thought of her son, the moon is following me, he would say, intrigued with himself & ignorant of size. The Foursquare Mission for the Glory of God, she heard him say, you may know of us? Oh yes, the woman's voice trails off—but that this great hump of land itself was moving, they with it, at only a greater sense of speed, under the likewise moving panoply of sky. History teaches us the ways of the Lord, he was saying, these Mayans now, great builders but—

History? she mutters to Yo, who is smiling out the window. Part of the landscape, he advises as the bus slows, entering another village, then pauses for a moment, though the doors do not open & no one gets on—this is a tourist bus, this is a sealed capsule on its way to a past it cannot understand. The voice, in its portentous confidence, booms on: overnight a whole civilization gone, & why? the experts don't know & no one thinks to look in the Bible. As the bus gets off to a slow start she concentrates on the adobe wall that barricades their passing from welltrodden dirt, from oval houses low & shady under orange trees, from bushes, chickens, a woman tending oven outdoors on the earth these animals, plants & people share, having nothing else. They from their glassedin perch can only stare, as

at the chicle hunters of the other bus they took, which stopped at
places a rag or sticks would mark, their driver knew, to look for,
stopped, & out they came from the dusty trails that stretch back into
nowhere, wrapped in their loose white pants, with knives, with hair
tied back, the chicle men who stand in the aisle barefoot, silent,
smelling of earth—they from their wellkept seats could only look at,
look at & thus transform to fit their views. We'll never escape ourselves, she thinks, & anger rises in her like a tide, she can feel it, filling
her head. You can thank the lord we're not part of their tour, Yo quips,
& she sees he has been watching her involvement, one eye on her,
ready to laugh.

  White mud stalls, more guidebooks, more Pepsi. A
battery of buses. They follow the others across to a gate, to the tour
groups milling around the open field—for it *is* a field, campo, held by
El Castillo august & dark against the cloudstrewn sky, tour groups
stream across. Deftly avoiding a man who insists they need a guide, Yo
heads for a small building at the back which she discovers on their map
as the Venus Platform, 'used for ceremonial dances.' The field is huge
& they, dwarfed by its imperial extent, are beginning to mill, she can
feel the confusion in him too, the book, which should be of some help,
is full of different visiting hours for various structures, & a linear map
she can't square with the actual ground they stand on, no compass
directions given, & at least twenty buildings they have to visit 'for a
complete tour of the zone.' Today she doesn't want to remember, & he
agrees, forget it, we can't cover everything.

  There, definitely, to one side
& ahead of them stands the temple they must move to, dark & head-
less against the sky boiling up, no blue now, nowhere to find the sun, a
temple with scores of columns supporting nothing, walls open to the
sky. What were they for? what did they hold up?

  Weaving in & out
around their four faces, she is woven into the mystery of the columns'
erased images, traces, of ochre at the feathery base of curving &
plumey lines, resolve, curiously, into a man: plumed helmet, shield, his

profile almost lost in the finery he wears, knight eagle, claws &
feathers at his feet, on others paws, knight jaguar—they who guard the
sun are still in attendance, however recessed into stone. At the top of
the stairs, not recessed at all but black against the shiftings of the sky,
giant free-standing snakes upend their tails, their impossible rattles
that surely must plummet, a thick column of serpent body, &, at her
feet, the monster head horned, plugged, plumed, its teeth rim an open
cavity curved like the roof of a mouth, mouth of a snake, invites
entry—Drawing back, she wonders how the columns offset their rattles
& looks for Yo to ask him but he is nowhere in sight, though she walks
to the top of the stairs & scans the field. Here a stone man lies with a
bowl on his belly—for the hearts of sacrificial victims the book says, &
with his head strained to one side, glares at her, guarding (or offering?)
the bowl. Everything is Toltec, opened out, exposed, & the softer more
intimate lines of Uxmal with its quiet huts commemorated in stone
seem far away. She descends & makes for the Thousand Columns
along one side—a market? colonnade? These, unlike the others, are
round & loosely mortared. From here the whole side of the temple can
be seen in relief, more warriors, more eagles & jaguars, all contained by
rippling lengths of snake, & above them, set in to a square motif of
feathers, the open head of a serpent reaches out of the stone toward
her, bearing a man's head in its throat—swallowed? appearing or
disappearing? like the sun—

Impressive isn't it! She turns, two Ameri-
cans, it is the tall gawky one in khaki pants & boots who spoke (still
enthusiastic, still in the field) now eyeing the head with a proprietary
look. Yes, she concurs. Satisfied, he nods & moves on, even as she
realizes, no, it isn't only that. & wanting to show Yo these snakes in all
their fearsomeness, thinking to find him further on, she heads into the
grass which is long here, little paths trailing off to less visible ruins.
Mounds, hillocks seeded over, grass like some curious pelt wavers in a
wind that is rising, sky lifting, huge & darkly lit, over this grass small
figures are lost in, reveals, the way it moves, these lines like hair rising
down a backbone, hidden ridges, spines of lost structure, hollows she

stumbles down—nothing she can trace. 'south colon-
nade . . . said to have been a market . . . east and north . . . steam bath.'
Words lift from the page into a sky that is huge & blow away. In the
silence surrounding her, rustles, feet in the grass, small noises murmur,
only to each other. A kind of panic seizes, she is lost & where is he,
this man who recognizes, knows again, returning them to where they
live. There is no one here. Hurriedly, she stumbles back toward that
great black pyramid at center.

Where he is, of course, Yo, himself,
at the edge of the grass involved in focusing. Seeing his preoccupation
she is envious for a moment, coming up, I thought you were over
there, waving her hand in the general direction of her absence. He
frees his eye & looks up buoyantly, I've used up half a roll on the
pyramid alone, the light is marvellous. & catching her look—just
consider it my way of seeing the ruins, come on, where shall we go?
It's not that, she might have said, losing it, lost, & thought, chi chén,
at the mouth of the well, with the stress on chén, at the mouth of the
well of the Itza. The well, she said. Cenote, empty, that was another
name for it.

A path, a road, broad & sandy, glimmers in the muffled
light of the sky as they traverse jungle on both sides, thornbush, no
flowers, though the people themselves suffice, clothing of different
colours, different skins—children chattering, & the women coming
back, full of it, though she can't tell exactly what they say. Even the
gawky archaeologist walks this way, reliving the old procession she
thinks, how many times has he made this trip?

At first there is only the
promontory of the old temple on its rim & then the deepening cliff
beyond, white limestone, astonishingly white, ringed & layered &
then, standing on the edge itself, they see water a long way down,
flecked with leaves like petals, a brackish green, utterly opaque.
Though leaves drift, wind barely blurs the surface, as if the water itself
were too heavy to move. So that's what they threw people into, he
says, no wonder they never came up. '. . . remains of thirteen men,

twentyone children, eight women' plus 'jade, gold & copper bells, copper sandal soles, etc.' a woman reads from her guidebook. It's a sinkhole, her companion explains loudly, limestone is full of caves you know, the water just drips & drips & the cave gets bigger & bigger & then one day, boom, there's a hole—you can see how they'd think it was magic. Not magic, she wants to say, no, not magic. White reamed sides water has cored insistently over the centuries, converge on the core itself, this lightflecked (gold dust), this rank depth nothing alters—simply sinks, down to where Chac dwells, & the drowned call, keep your face down, let me tell you . . . It was an honour, the guide's explaining, she can hear his voice, patient, as if he were telling again the two girls in shorts who stand not quite believing: this sacrifice was an honour you see—they were dressed in fine clothes like brides, & heavy jewellery, heavy inside too—it was a feast day & they drank much wine, & so in the water they sank, you understand, abajo, like a stone. One of the girls questions him sceptically: you mean they didn't struggle? they just willingly went to their deaths? He is patient, after all they are Norteamericanas: no they didn't die, they went to the rain god with messages from all the people & this was very important, they went down to the house of Chac. The girl persists: you mean that's what they were told, but surely when they saw someone struggling they'd think oh maybe this was a mistake, this person doesn't want to die. With dignity the guide went on: after they jumped all the people turned their backs & they threw in something precious of their own. Oh! so they wouldn't see them! the girl insists to her friend. These were the things the explorer Edward Thompson found at the bottom, many beautiful carved things of jade & copper, many offerings to Chac—

   All legend, Yo whispers into her listening ear, even Edward Thompson, all stories of the place. & in part she knows what he means, how that is not the light breeze blowing his shirt against his chest, her hair against her skin, & these, together with the stone behind them, form a real continuum they keep walking down, walking the path again, shifting the limestone sand that puffs up over their

dusty feet. Still, she says, they are part of the place & how can we see it
without understanding them? Oh but we see it, he says, however we
do, you know that. But, but—sinkhole, the word keeps echoing, abajo,
like a stone.

       After the Tzompantli, incised with double row of skulls on
posts, after a frieze of plumed warriors, after the Chacmool with his
bowl for hearts, they enter the ball court where long stone walls
bounce back the heat onto shrivelled grass. Various tour groups are
being shown long carved panels on the walls. Two stone rings high up
through which the ball must be thrown, teams of seven players, padded
uniforms (how could they play in this heat?)—the guide of the group
they stand near is short but she can hear his voice even if she can't see
him: here we have a man kneeling & you can see that he has lost his
head, behind him stand the six remaining members of his team, now
who is this man? A fellow beside her shouts: the captain of the losing
team. Ah that is what you might think, my friend, but you are wrong.
It is not the captain of the losing team but the captain of the winning
team! Yes—(over murmurs of surprise, even, she feels it, disbelief) in
those days they did things differently. To us it would be unthinkable
but to them, no, this man won the right to sacrifice, this man went off
to the gods. Look, you see the blood spouting from his neck here? you
see how these streams of blood turn into flowers?

                            How do you know
this, she wants to shout, every account she has read records that the
loser was sacrificed. Has he made it up? & yet his sense of it agrees with
the man at the well. Is this a native conspiracy to make history look
good? & is she any the less 'Northamerican' than these others who
likewise cannot conceive of a man fighting to *lose* his life. Cult of the
warrior, part of her says, invented by men to make death bearable. But
another part of her murmurs, wait, wait, this is something you can't
translate, not even the words are right. Not lose, he didn't fight to *lose*,
he fought to win, the right, he said, to sacrifice, to make, sacred (what
does that word mean?) he fought for the right, she would start again, to
give up a life, where blood, is blood—

Lost in thought again? he had come up & put his arm around her & she was grateful for that, for the presence of it, firm against her neck as his reminder, if we want to see the other zone we'd better get moving you know, time's running on. & it was, is, as they are, she can feel that now, striding with him over the open field that darkens as they cross it, not lost, directive in their going, past the monument that dwarfs these people swarming toward its promise of time somehow contained there—All she can feel is the moving, rhythm of her limbs in step with his, wind blowing against their skin, & the day, ominous of rain, a storm, an exultation of movement—they are in the middle of, alive.

More buses waiting, white with purple & crimson stripes, irrelevant now as they cross the highway onto another path, set off by stick fences, into windblown foliage where a woman crouches by the root of a tree, her butterfly huipils she is selling pinned from a line between two branches. & she who lives here looks at them as they pass, selling & not selling, squatting in an earth she knows cannot surprise her. It is the same earth the stones of a pyramid on their right have tumbled into, nothing more than a giant mound bushes climb up through, but as the path opens they see, rising to conclude it, the massive face of Las Monjas, sprawling congery of temples in several stages, & to their left on a rise of steps, the singular broken hump of El Caracol, shellcoiled observatory, hermetic & solid against the billowing sky. Little bushes they stop to eat an orange by & stare: it is both Mayan & Toltec, organic upthrust of stone in the jungle. People hurry by in the gathering wind. She leaves their orange peels in a small cluster at the foot of the bush & they head for the stone steps where he takes a picture, but she hurries on, drawn to that stone coiling wound in on itself, an ascent she can see through part of the wall, the stairs, it is broken, the seal is broken & the inner stairs climb halfrevealed to starholes at the top.

A curving trench in the shape of a crescent greets her feet as they reach the platform, she enters the door, enters the stony dark to face a wall that forces her around, along with the others, a curving passageway which, just at the point where its bend allows a glimpse of the outside light from the next entry, breaks, midway, with another doorway onto a second & even more inward passage, likewise curving & even more coiled upon the heart of the building itself, that central shaft which rises up in the dark, housing the stairs, invisible from here. Moving slowly through the curved recesses of the place, she feels like a mote, forced with the flow of these other motes, since the passage is so narrow none can pass but all must follow, along some duct, some coiled vesicle of a body that in its thickness contains them all. Swallowed, she thinks, not snail but serpent coiled on itself, & looking for the doors discovers them so spaced that those of the second wall fall always *between* those of the first & there is never, at least from the inner passage, direct access to the outdoors, while the shaft itself seems to contain no entry at all. Now she has come across a clot in the flow, a small group gathered around the voice of a guide, a voice she'd heard & thought was only another tourist, but sees now, though again she can't see him (why are they always so short, she thinks, or is it we who are so tall?) that he has stopped his group at a particular spot in the coil & is pointing upward to a hole she had missed, up in the dark the grey light from doorways doesn't dissipate, above their heads. That is how they gained the stairs, he says, or what she can make of his Spanish says, it was covered by a cloth & reached by a small ladder, but they have taken the ladder away, he is sorry, es peligroso, no one can go up, but then, he adds, it was forbidden to all but the priests to enter this most sacred heart.

Ah so that is where they watched the movements of the moon, of Venus, that was where they located themselves in the windings of the cosmos & only there did they know the darkening that was about to descend, a dangerous knowledge. She feels suddenly trapped in the peopled air, the containment of this stone & moves, almost runs, quickly through the nearest grey, into the outer passage & then along it to a bright door. Even cloudy light is brilliant out where the wind blows, out in the streaming shifting, forcing her eyes to open into the day, which *has* grown darker, yes, rain is beginning to pit the stone, from the west, she can feel wet drops, & looking back, sees suddenly that the four outer doors must face the cardinal points, & the inner ones some points between, while what is left of doors or starholes at the top look also north east south west—the outer sphere of the building keyed one way, the way the world lies, the inner keyed another.

Those inner doorways form, not a cross then but an x, x marks the spot, that point, points outward on the horizon, sunrise, sunset, summer zenith, winter descent, converge: four zones of the earth turn green at their meeting, that fifth point, visible only as a hidden stairwell.

4 – NIGHT (MERIDA

It wasn't the moon—you're quiet tonight, he'd said, as they lay there—& it wasn't the usual sense of night, she could recapture that by letting her eye see its tall gloom, pale light from their shuttered doors, fan making a blur up there though its sound continued an obvious clank & whirr. no, that's easy, easy to get back to, what she's trying to recapture is her earlier thought of him & where that put them.

i can't remember, she admits, something i understood, or thought i did, about you, no, not you, where you are. it was at the old site & then i went looking to find you & by the time i did there was something else. you were looking at that little building with the frieze, he says, i remember you talking about four animals above the doorway you said were brothers, four something, a Mayan word, they hold up the sky—

the four bacabs. something slid quietly into place, so quiet she almost missed it. the plane of the earth where earth folds into sky, at the four corners earth falls into, colours & trees & serpent-monsters— they stand for disappearing points. that is the furthest she or anyone can go. except at centre, where the central tree grows upward & down, the observatory—stay with up, movement of star & moon, movement of sun, its faces each step of the way—she can't stay there because she sees him, the shoeshine man has surfaced with that thought, she sees him slumped there, under those trees, & begins to remember . . . (i can't drive)

what do you understand? he laughs, poking a quick finger in her ribs. no, wait, she says, it has to do with your fascination for the shoeshine man. which one? you know, the one who is dying. she half expects him to disagree with that summation of what he means to them, & he does say, you mean the one who is always there? yes. he's not *my* fascination you know (a package wrapt & tied on the driver's seat), he's yours, you're the one who remembers him (a package in her lap). that's true, she thinks, is it? flashing back over the times he has recurred in their conversation, sitting between them: she thought he had brought him there, but it was her, she thought he had spotted him on the periphery, sitting on the edge of the square, but suddenly at center, under a mass of leafy dark, his right arm (she has stumbled on him) coiled about him, pulling the jacket to, fingers on the left gone numb, gone dead, & music, insipid out of electric wires, frail & faraway, a familiar version of soledad, the sun's gone dead, nine crazy moons jumping all over space—is it nine? is it number nine? (is that your number? she got out of the car to fix its turning, it is six, six—not yet, she said, not knowing there were nine steps down—he was right behind her,

or so she thought, but when she turned in the glimmering light, he had gone, & no one ahead, only this unfamiliar road— intending what? the sun will not depart, it is waiting for someone, & they mark, these silent ones, life suspended, there in its going, in the long extended entry into the dark, they walk its rim & watch, their own disappearance? or the disappearance of those who come?

she'd

thought they simply marked the ground of her dream, that native family who said she'd better go—the power of the sea & the power of dwarfs, they said, are working together—now she knows who they are, how they preside over the sun's going & initiate her in her own departure, lords of the turning of light to dark who live where absence is, at the mouth—

she isn't ready, no not yet, she will cling to num- bers, to any evidence of their presence to each other, she will not be tricked, she will stay where the world is & they are all together,

&

turning to him, calling him back from his own fastness of solitude she asks, where are you? nowhere he says. you must be somewhere. to which there is no reply, or there is, depending on what he means by nowhere. come back, she whispers into his ear, that's no place to be. oh ho, he rolls over, his arm unfolding out of the dark to pull her in, you'll change even nowhere into some place, won't you? as he laughs at her need to be here, laughs to make her realize the impossibility of what they nevertheless give their otherwhere up to: the laughing insistency of skin, warm to each other, the only reply she might make, wordless, is in the weight their bodies do press against the dark, as they, both of them, move into the closeness that is their felt selves, present at last.

      & the wing of his hair falls across her face, a dark odour usually pulled tight to him released, so that she enters an inner room made of his smell, the skin of his neck, hidden inside that fall, the wet hole of his mouth—even as her tongue rinds his, back of, inside his teeth, arousing his insistency, she falls away, or floats—no, his body brings hers forward, making, in its suck at nipples, in the stroke of buttocks her hand gathers, handfuls of flesh, to reach, sip, take, become, come in her skin calls to his, bones raised in an arc of desire, starlike, singularity to be resolved, dissolved now as he enters, *they* do, a confusion of entering of flowing out to him, to heat, the heat of him inside is her surrounding (him) is their surrounding element, a liquid entry as they somewhere, having lost ground, roll & ship, warmth / weight / wet, no, sinking into it, to, slip that element, yes he is coming, yes she is flying, right. straight. through.

      o the shudderings & shiftings body makes, & settles, having come through again. come to here again. (hey we're back again) only the recognition of their, in fact, presence to each other, & the mutuality of that, the actual heaviness of his head on her breast as, no doubt, her flesh to his face—read for a moment in the smile he gives, she answers, before fading, before rolling over into, separate. sleep.

      a little start, a little twitch, of all direction,

lost, to sink back into (mothering) night, it, lets us float (not wet but dark, mother—no stars, no calendars & wheels, mother—a little seed, a little dark, fruit—dark, a long way down, & there is no horizon elsewhere which the owls fly escort to, the ends of earth, that edge where sky descends—

in the dark of the light i am above, the light is at the furthest edges, in the dark, in the not quite dark, caskets glimmer, large at the shoulder & pointed towards the feet, they are white in the dark of a silvery wood that is weathered, in triples, like leaves, so shallow scarcely graves, stones topple crooked, above, not in, dry ground, long gone, no one to say what's broken open, whose remnants of cloth torn, into the dark they've drained—at the furthest (was i looking?) is the newest, at the end of the others, more white, it glimmers, out of or in that dark. set it straight, they say, it must be aligned with the others & i must drop down, pull—it will not—so, take hold of the nearest, pull—it rots, its rim, tears open & my hand, my arm, i, fall

into the night. fall (apart) into that flesh self creeps from. no, NOT to feel it, run, run straight through (home?) to get away from

i am running, running, it runs behind me, that horror (it will touch) get home, get home, through, the door & into, humming, house (no house i recognize) is full of relations—mother!—& the place is dark,

they come out to meet me, twins in yellow dresses, so you've come, cousins, smiling, you've come to the party after all —they thought i wouldn't, they thought i would stay up where they haven't— just, fresh, raw with it (don't touch me) pushing by to reach her, mother, who is busy with them all who come, i see from the doorway, who stay here, the dead, she queens it over them, this is her house & i have come in error—

turning to steal away, i hear her voice move out of that cavern to stay me, warning 'I don't want to lose that one too.'

so

64 GHOST WORKS

i know who it is i run from through the dark grown thicker than dark,
thick with will, it pulls me, pulls at my running, toward, to get to,
upward, to become, i can't, from this horizon, separate & rigid lying,
lean down toward me where i come, up from the dark to be her: you
must. come back. i am. into the day we live in i've become—myself
who sits up wildly awake beside him warm & heavily breathing & still
sleeping on.

MERIDA

On the other side of the square, they are, we are, he is saying, on the side of the square we never sit on, morning, swallows the zócalo, filled with it, that light ease light pours, into at centre (hole), pole they are taking the xmas tree down, no more lights, daytime dead outline of what was, at night, a coloured fantasy, but the tinsel wreaths still swing, looping across paths that ray out from that spot their eyes are fixed on, still, he is right, we are, on the side we never sit on, & though morning swallows, in its bright freshening of day, all that night lets run, strange currents, vampire bats at the movie house, or the laughing seductive strays, giving way to the world, teenage derelicts at midnight play around the original derelict himself swept, even he swept out by morning, its shallows, leaving them all a little beached, the paltry litter of yesterday, light raying through the indian laurel, their old trunks' tatter whitewash adrift in peels, the balloon man goes slowly by, trailing pinks & blues, through a trickle of hose, someone's watering, halfhearted, gone off for coffee, gone off into the morning scatter through the day, knowing, even the gardener knows, how one must splay out, simply, to be here & not—it's not the zócalo, it's not the morning swallowing, it's night, under the o so solid scatter of these pavingstones, dark clings, & she must not, step into that house again—

Did you see him, she says (can you keep me here?), the shoeshine man on the other side of the square, we must have passed him on our way here, though she had actually forgotten to look. No, he says, I didn't, but the blind man's there, & she could see him inching his way along the wall to change position, all day with his hand out, blind faith, not the scrawnier hand of the dwarf woman in the sidestreet who, humped in a doorway, massiveness of that flesh between her shoulders somehow packaging all that was absent from her legs, begged with a kind of bitter grimace (still knew how to curse, 'encountered on a journey to the west,' they said, 'old mannikins') who'd marked their journey in the dream, even before they left, & now she is here it is something else, *her* journey not theirs, he, living out in the street, on the square, sees earth for what it is, a vast terrain, these people here, sloped on benches or walking, these women, these cabdrivers, passing the time of day, it pools, it shallows here, she wants to stay, play, insist, this is not west, but east they have moved to, the fact of it, we sit with our backs to the sea, we are facing south, all day lightens the air before us, we are facing into the yellow earth, toward the men of yellow corn, so the muralist had said in the building behind them, held in the palm of the bacab of the south (it is warm here, it is safe)—'así pintó el Mayab eterno Fernando Castro Pacheco'

& she who must struggle to come up out of the dark, out of the west, they say is black or, coming from north, a white they do not know, of invisible bodies on visible streets, those cleaner colder roads we walk, spectral or absent, where no one lives behind the eyes that skim by: that is a kind of hell

—she came up from, with owls, she came up out of the nine dark worlds of bolon tiku, & left, no not her father, lord of death, but mother—why does it change, why does the dream change it like that? He has taken his arm away from the back of the bench to light a match, his hand curved to protect the flame. I had a dream, she says, last night, so vivid I can't seem to leave it behind—Go on, he says. I was flying over a graveyard, at least I think I was flying, looking for a new coffin which was at the very end. It was out of line with the two beside it & I was supposed to straighten it but when I bent over to do that I realized I had to hang on to the middle one to give myself enough leverage & when I did my hand went through it was so rotten & felt myself fall into the darkness of it. I was running through the dark to get home but when I got there the house was full of people, I could hear voices in the kitchen where I knew my mother was but twins of my cousin, I mean they were my cousin but twins, came into the hall to greet me, only I didn't want to see anyone so I turned to go & then I heard her voice from the kitchen call out 'I don't want to lose that one too!' I ran terrified, trying to get back here, it was as if I was separate from my body, it seemed to take an extraordinary effort to get back into myself, to get back beside you & wake up.

Even telling it, terror clouds the edges of her telling & yet, now she has told it it isn't like it was, the telling fixes it in a way that wasn't felt then, a map that doesn't quite fit the terrain she was running through, doesn't take him back to that terrain the dark inhabits but like the square they are sitting in, on the same bench in the mutual day, occupies them. Not that she had meant it to take over the day, obscuring bench, trees, the balloon man, but now she can't take it back & a little embarrassed waits for him to survey it, the cigarette flaring between his fingers like a small signal. She had expected him to laugh, to make some joke, placing it thus in a waking perspective she might also enter. She has wanted him to say, as she has said to her own child on his waking, it's only a dream. But this morning he is quiet, thinking, & then he looks at her: so you went to visit your mother, he says. She hadn't thought of it as voluntary, as a 'visit,' but as a descent, perhaps she had sought out? & was that her mother? Mothers live on the earth in the day, one ascends out of the dark to mother, that's what all the stories say—but then the stories, the old stories, are always told in somebody else's language, & we don't really know. She's everybody's mother, he says, mother earth. She laughs, oh but *who* is that? *she* was definitely someone. You just met her, he says.

& the falling begins, o the horror of falling into, earth, in that we are alone—she had wanted him to pave it over, into nothing more than leaf play on paving stone, a surface she or anyone might walk across—she hadn't wanted to be alone,

. . . ¿hamaca? a voice says, only one hundred fifty pesos, special price
for you, henequèn, very good, & the end of a pink doubleply hammock
is tossed into her lap, thickly coiled end ring nestling in her skirt, look,
he says, a boy, no more than a boy, nodding at her briskly, I show you,
& he fans it out for her, the henequèn slivering & filming between
them & separating finally into a pink & white fan extending six feet
across the stones between his hand & hers. Matrimonio, he says, for
two, & nods at the man beside her. She looks at Yo who laughs, who is
already, in the way he sits back, dissociating himself from this exchange (she hadn't asked for—& their talk, o what about their talk?) It
is to her the boy has made his advance, though they have turned away
other salesmen, the square infested with them (always a quick resentment at their fixing them so obviously as 'marks') having agreed they
would not spend what money they had on a hammock, still something
about the way this boy hovers, not carrying on in the usual manner,
not even accompanied by a mate (as, usually, they worked the square
in pairs, these hamaca men) not, obviously, out to talk them into
buying but in some way waiting as he hovers there, that makes her
almost want to give in—but no, she says, we don't need a hammock.
Good price, he insists, but as if on the fact of it, you get nowhere else.
No, she says, gracias, as he loops it toward him, deftly taking it from
her lap in the last fold. ¿Habla español? Un poco. From where you
come? he asks, setting his bundle of hammocks on the stone beside
their bench & sitting on it next to her. Canada. So glib, the answer to
that question, but what might make sense across the divide he is trying
to bridge—up north? beyond the United States? how far does his sense
of north extend? She lets it rest & is surprised when he says, On-tahr-
io? Of course, hamaca man. Another part of Canada, she says, the
West Coast, on the sea, & points, roughly, to where she thinks the
Pacific might be. He is taking a small notebook out of his back pocket,
¿y su marido? what, ¿perdón? hus-ban? he points, she hesitates (¿mi
amigo? with his eyes set across the square, who is there already, butting
his cigarette for a stroll, with camera, through sun & shadow, forms on
benches, all that is out there she returns from, to this insistency) yes?

What country? Canada too, & divining his curiosity adds, Japanese-Canadian. ¡Ah! Japonés, he scans Yo's retreating back & gestures at the book, you write for me, en Inglés? Taking the stubby pencil, she sees as he flicks through searching for a space, that it is full of words & that the writing differs, some words printed in big letters, some written phrases, some Spanish, some English. I learning Inglés, he looks up seriously, people write me & I learning the words—esta, la señora de On-tahr-io, she write me. The words he is pointing to say, 'take the freeway' & below that, 'north-south.' Freeway, he says, his finger under the word, stocky & vivid on the much handled page, hand of a farmer, broad palmed, no hamaca salesman, hands that are used to making, & suddenly, as if from some dusk, his body comes forward under the pale blue shirt, sneakers, red billed baseball cap, a young man's insistence, quiet, but humming there beside her, silent & waiting.

His eyes are on the page, as hers, & out of the force between them she asks the question, what are freeways? He audibly answers, she say me, in America, in Canada too, el camino, big trucks, much cars, go very fast very far. Of course, she thinks, & no, she thinks, you go very far here too. But how can she say that? what right has she? Me, I want to know it, he is saying, so I learning Inglés. But why? (perhaps he wants to see America like she wants to see Mexico?) He looks at her scornfully (no it is different) hamaca, he shrugs & gestures broadly across the square. Tixkokob my village, I live with my mother & father, my brothers, is small village, fifty kilómetros from Mérida En la mañana las hamacas, he smacks the bundle he is sitting on, en la noche, las hamacas—I sell two maybe three, no good, ¿m'entiende? not much money.

It is so clear the way he sees it, lucid as a map, but she, doubting on the far side of it, sees him lost there, the freeway of his imagination snarled in immense complications he has no vision of. It isn't only size, or only speed, what can she say? that the duplicity of map & terrain, that maps are something we are good at, countries in themselves, unreal, but perfectly believable, until one tries to set foot there & the land falls away—

Glancing around she catches sight of Yo at the heart of the zócalo facing one way & shooting down the path that leads to the eastern edge—las lluvias olorosas' (was it promise? hope?) There is nothing she can say, he lives where he lives & will carry that with him in a way she can't foresee. And grinning sideways at her he says suddenly, first I see México, & she knows he means the capital, whence all roads lead, & which is just as far away. I learning Inglés, you teach me? tapping at the book. Sí. Insistence will get him there. El Inglés es difícil, ¿no? En mi escuela—¿como se dice? School? Sí, school, I learning Spanish—What do you speak at home? she guesses in the same instant, Mayan? Sí, Maya. Now I help my family pero en mi escuela, they have teach to me the words, to write, ¿m'entiende? El Español no es difícil, mira: el día, same ¿m'entiende? pero en Inglés, este, ¿de? como se deletrea de? ¿De? (from what?) oh! day, d-a-y, she spells it out for him. Sí, sí, es difícíl. (This boy, who speaks Mayan, for whom Spanish is a second language, who is trying to teach himself English phonetically, is ready to take on North America—plunked beside her on his bundle of hammocks, 'henequèn, very good.')

Y este, he says, tapping the book, ¿qué es r-e-y-l? Reyl? He says something in Spanish, something she doesn't understand though she gathers it's a word picked up from dos Americanos, & staring at it suddenly she gets it, rail! (of course, distance again) Sí sí, reyl, ¿que es reyl? It is what a train runs along, a railroad, do you know that word? Reyl ro? please. She writes it for him in his book, sounding it out, ra-il ro(a)-d, the a, this letter, doesn't have a sound, just o, ro-d. She thinks to tell him about the sign RR, that intersection of rail & road, which after all he will know (a disappearing car) but that might complicate it for him (he who is separate, who in his Mexican version of American clothes, in his Mayan skin, comes out of some village to the east, separate & solid). No, he insists, los Americanos gave him the word & they did not say it was a train. What else could it be? rail? railing? something you hold onto? she enquires, looking around for one, sees Yo a few yards away, pointing the camera at them, & calls, what could rail mean besides railroad & railing? Ranting & railing? he laughs, an impish laugh. That's too complicated. Oh well you know I don't know English (I can't drive, he said. The package bundled up & set aside, beside him on the seat there, & separate. Wait, he would set off into that strange terrain without it, & she must stop him. Or was it her? Wait—he did not speak, or he said, they knew how to depict expression certainly, & then their iron heads rose up, scowling or grinning, out of that earth, & it was her who had brought them there—what does it mean?) ¿Qué quiere decir?—reyl? (not even a photograph can rescue them) Rule? she says, Royal? (whose rule? how get at that?) No, no (he digs away, the little man with pickaxe) something else (it was 'the power of'?)

Oigame, he tries again, reyl, REY—L. Oh! (the pronunciation) you mean REAL? Sí sí, his face breaks into that smile, & they are there, they have hit it. ¿Qué es reel? he calls it into question (& is this real? any of of it? their ground has fallen away & she is falling, how speak to that with her impoverished Spanish, his broken English?—help, it is instinct, she looks around for Yo & spots him in the centre of the square again (what is he doing?) shooting west, place of the sun's going, place of evil winds, hunger, death—this is her undertaking, this is what she must come up from. Real means actual, means, here (she slaps the bench), a thing, here (no dawning) verdad. ¿Verdad? ¿sí? (What is the Spanish & suddenly it dawns on her, but isn't it?) En Espanõl, real, (rey-ál) ¿no? ¡Ah sí, sí auténtico! What? I mean ¿qué? Auténtico. Authentic! yes (he knows that word. Always it is pronunciation gets in the way, they have the same words, unrecognized, he asking her for the English she thought he hadn't known, already knowing the word she hadn't recognized. But what was the question then? What is real? (reyl, some Texan speech)—Auténtico he said (in the author's own hand).

Astonished, she glances up, sees Yo still at the heart of the zócalo, turned now, towards them. She wonders is he taking them or taking what stretches all around them, they only

points in the whole, sees, suddenly, him seeing herself grown small
with this stranger, from whom, with whom a real conversation sprouts,
between them, like the trees they sit under, live among. What is your
name? she asks. Manuel. Will you write it? & taking the back of the
dictionary she offers, he prints

$$M A R ve L \quad J E S u S$$

that Spanish use of Christ's name, but
why not? power name, she thinks, any one might have, saviour, &
connects, Manuel, Emmanuelle—wasn't it, god is with us? His hand
continues to mark, abrupt strokes against the white:

$$P E c h \qquad P A T$$

so that they form a
square—these two, names from a language she doesn't recognize,
printed beneath those two of heaven. Pech, mi padre, Pat, mi madre,
he explains, en Inglés, you write only the name of the father, no? Pero,
además, you are the child of your mother, ¿m'entiende?

ground, he is
saying, his or anyone's. under heaven, earth. what she had wanted to
overlook, that dark, that other self she has fought up through. he
comes to the edge of, telling her how it lies, horizon, what they are
bound by. But where do you live? she asks, ¿su dirección?

He writes,

$$D o N M i c i L i o$$

house,
but spells it, 'don,' gift, house

$$C o N o c i d o$$

known, he writes, is known (give up you
know) this house you fight up through, at centre, dark, hole at the
heart of the field, 'thup,' little one, where the world disappears,
reaching up through the dark, through mother & up, this branching

growth, gift—('in my father's house are many mansions')

When she looks from the words to his eyes they are cast
down, busy under the shadow of the baseball cap with the page on
which he continues to print

cA LlC 2 1
A CPŞ A 13 6
7'í x Ko Ko b
Y Lc M ß X

Mi dirección, he smiles, returning them to
earth, where they sit on a bench, in the heart of, handing back the
book (but wait)—¡Allá! ¡mi amigo! loitering several yards away, who
calls, ¿cómo le va? with a nod at her as Manuel shrugs, & slipping the
notebook into a back pocket, es un vendedor muy bueno, mi amigo,
standing up, tipping the baseball cap at her, adiós señora, hammocks
slung over his shoulder, he joins his friend & fades back into the day.

Or

their day (El Mayab) out in the square (es la tierra) the men with xmas
tree lights have got them down & left, the others stay, much as they
have done, slumped on benches or halfturned watching passersby. Sun
falls silently all around them. From a sky advanced to noon the white-
washed trunks of indian laurel bear up masses of glossy leaves against—
four corners light & shadowy, these trees make of themselves, among,
light bearing down (misterioso y antigua), she sees Yo coming from
across the square, she sees him walk, quick & almost light, almost
disappearing into the ones he walks among, this man with whom she
shares the day, whose face, alight with question, singular in that field
that lights all ways—she takes her eyes from his, embarrassed by the
distance—not them, they dark against its lighting—eyes slide back to,
making of them in the way dark lights them, shining, showing forth
what each one is, each of them in the night they also rise up from, in
which everything speaks—well? he will say, did you learn any Mayan?—
into the... (silence).

MONTH OF
HUNGRY GHOSTS

We cannot retrace our steps, going forward may be
the same as going backwards —

Gertrude Stein
22nd July 1976
Bangkok 8:00 A.M.

Arendt : The Human Condition .

MONTH OF
HUNGRY GHOSTS

Snakes. Woke up dreaming of the striking head of a cobra—pok—
into me, my hand over breast. Snakes at the Temple of the Reclining
Buddha where we stopt, latter part of the floating market tour. A snake
pit, the "doctor" a young Thai in boots & white medical jacket, who
poked at the snakes with stick, getting them to raise their heads, spread
their hoods—cobras all colours from black to brown but with same
diamond markings on hood. He'd pick up one by tail, slap it on table,
poke it til erect & facing him, ready to strike, then wd fascinate it with
one hand as he went with the other for its neck, grabbed, just below
head, immediately flattening hood. Assistant handed him flat dish
which he inserted in cobra's mouth, forcing the edge of it back against
the jaw & poison glands (you could hear the teeth scraping on the
plastic) & squeezing the head so that drops of poison were forced out
onto the plate—transparent liquid. Poison goes to victim's heart &
stops it, the announcer (an old grinning Thai with dirty turban &
microphone in hand) announced, "and our doctor never misses, he is
very quick, he has to be."

Then yesterday in the Temple of the Emerald Buddha (Wat Phra
Keo) on the palace grounds, our guide pointed out a picture of Buddha
sitting under a tree, his body wrapt in the coils of a snake & his head
canopied by the 7 heads of the snake, a nagah, watersnake. When he
sought enlightenment by meditation under the baobab tree, he vowed
not to move, even though it rained so hard the rain came up to his
navel & after a week of sitting the watersnake wrapt itself around him,
holding its 7 heads over him to protect him & at that point he gained
enlightenment. That's why, guide said, Thai temples always corner

their roofs with heads of snakes, as protection (flaming? crests I'd thought). To be wrapt in that other, that so non-human & not suffer revulsion but see the snake's gift of protection—must be what we call "grace."

Sitting on the floor of the temple with us, our guide slid quietly from politics to religion, a spontaneous sermon. A Thai who'd had the usual Buddhist training including 3 months as "yellow man" (monk), has for the last 4 yrs been studying Mormon teachings & teaches in the Mormon church. "Maybe you go by bus & you go by train & I go by plane but the important thing is our destination & that is the same point." A dualist, said Christ (pronounced Kreest) gives men a choice as to whether they follow him or not & so he stands for good in the world but Satan says you must follow me if you want power. Said that young men as monks are all taught to meditate & that meditation "makes you happy because you do not want food or clothes or objects, you are all the time happy inside " & that when you have meditated a lot you leave the city which is full of "objects" & go to the jungle where you have nothing because that is where you are happy.

He referred to the division amongst the Thai people between those who wanted the Americans to leave & those who didn't. Said the Govt officially wanted them to go but actually didn't "because they make corruption with them." Our afternoon guide spoke of the student upheavals, students pro-Communist & the rest of the people against them. The student headquarters, communist headquarters in Bangkok, had been burned. Police headquarters also burned to the ground. Said people didn't like Communists & if they2 were invaded would repel them: "We love our king." (how much of this is made-to-order propaganda?) But he also said the first democratization in 1932 when the absolute monarchy became a constitutional monarchy was sham & it's only been recently, as a result of protest, that real democratization has occurred.

The temples, their ornate imagery, colours, gilt, such a contrast to the rusted corrugated iron & wood shacks most of the people live in, live very simply, poorly ("we know no mattresses & pillows," our guide said yesterday, "only wood to sleep on," speaking of how poor the country is for bodily comforts— "inside we have enough, but not outside for our bodies.") It's the calm in the temples, & the sense of many lives invested there—candles burning constantly, incense, flowers, food offerings, gilt leaf offerings pasted onto images & statues (temples are USED here), the strange displays of sacred power such as the 40 yr old body of the 20 yr old nun who'd died of malaria, displayed in all her white muslin garb, faded jasmine wreaths, skull on bent head visible, flesh of hand wrinkled & dark as if embalmed. Her not rotting seen as the sign of her spirituality—

Buddhism here in all its ritualism & ceremony honours the flowering of the body, even in deprivation, as it points to its invisibility—the tension of the 2 seen as the tension of life.

22nd July
Penang 11:30 PM

A cheecha running along the ceiling above makes a funny chirping noise—light brown almost pink legs, one beady eye upon me writing at this glasstopped desk. Waves of cricket & treefrog sounds continuously breaking outside around the house. Barking dogs in the distance. Hot. Dark.

Once out on the road by myself, walking down it—vague memories of walking down it as a child, knew where the golf course was where we used to pick mushrooms in the early morning—once out in that humming dark, the trees—one I did seem to know, spreading its great umbrella arms (sam-cha? the same?) writhing in the light (streetlamp), it's the *vivid*ness of everything here—I was afraid, had to force myself to walk—afraid of this life & what the night hides, bats? cobras? At the last house on the road (such huge gardens around each mansion) a tall frangipani tree dropping white blossoms on the grass (which isn't grass but a kind of low growing broadleafed plant). I came back to find Mr. Y in his pyjamas & Dad outside looking for me. Locking up. Then a to-do about locking the ironwork gate in the upper hall that separates the bedrooms from the rest of the house ("we've had a spot of trouble"). . .

Mr. Y moves like water in a conversation, either rushing forward with endless talk of company affairs or receding into not hearing much else. A habit of not directly answering questions, the servants do that too. Very kind. The old world courtesy, the constant talking about a thing to be done while doing it, the concern over little things like leaving a door open or closed—Yeat's lapis lazuli old man with a touch of the absurd. His passion is business, he's full of gossip about all the people whose lives have been involved with the company to any extent—& all the internal dissensions, inner politics—absorbing, the game business is, played with utter seriousness. He hints at many things yet overstates, "it was cruel" etc., which makes for a curious style of conversation.

Eng Kim: recognized her as soon as I saw her, but curiously didn't want to show my recognition immediately. She's hardly changed at all—so amazingly similar in appearance after 25 years. Still that almost shy, perfectly naive sweetness—how can she have lived these years so apparently untouched? She's "worked for the bank" (i.e. looked after the bank manager & family) most of the time. The perfect servant, neat & unassuming, quiet as a shadow—yet I catch a glint of humour in her smile. Will it be possible to know her better? It's so strange to be, now 25 years later, someone she serves, instead of the child she chivvied along.

O the disparities—how can I ever relate the two parts of myself? This life would have killed me—purdah, a woman in—the restrictions on movement, the confined reality. I can't stand it. I feel imprisoned in my class—my? This is what I came out of. & how else can I be here?

disparities

Song River
Cafe cuttle-
fish

    dried flesh
    in the dark

    shine

water's edge

    old bay
    new road

    strange
    fish

res publica

each his own
how each does chant
his tributary note
to the great cantata
under the raintrees'
'thrice-canopied'

      chirrup

cedes to the
trinng • trinng • trinng
bare feet pedal into
oblivion

General sweeping going on—the kabun seems to sweep the grounds each day. sound of bamboo broom. chink of china (discreet) from kitchen. birds woke me at 7:00 with a tide of music. the old fans work well, our room cool all night tho thick with humidity.

How can I write of all this? what language or what structures of language can carry this being here?

Flying in yesterday it was the size of the island that surprised me, not one hill but many, a range, all steeply wooded, overgrown. & Georgetown itself white in the sun, highrise crested now, sprawling. We came down from such a high altitude so fast the pain in my ears brought tears: the cost of re-entry? into the past?

Saturday the 24th

I have too much energy for this life, its do-nothing style—no real work to use storedup food energy. Always eating here: breakfast, lunch, dinner with tea (a meal in itself) in between. Then everyone goes to bed at 10:30. I want to get out, see the life not visible from these confines of a wellrun household. But how do it on my own? Even last night's walk with Pam down Jalan MacAllister brought us a car full of young men keeping pace with us asking if we want a ride, etc. & today Idris warns us as he lets us off for shopping alone to hang onto our purses. Tonight I have to ask Ah Yow to unlock the back door to let me in because I went out to record the chorus of frogs down the road after the house had been locked (they lock us in when they go off duty—a sealed fortress).

I'm finding out more about the taboos I was raised with, the unspoken confines of behaviour, than I am about Penang. Still, that's useful—it makes me see the root of my fears: either I obey the limitations & play safe, stay ignorant, or else I go off limits, play with "danger" & suffer the price of experience, wch is mostly unconscious anxiety that all the dire things prophesied will happen!

Saw a watersnake today in the brook I'd planned to wade down, see where it goes—about 3 ft long, striped in bands of brown & gold on black, coiling & uncoiling along the muddy edges of the stream rushing thick & fast with yesterday's rainy torrents. Snake again signals offlimits, danger to me. I can't get past the snakes in my life.

Went to market this morning with Ah Yow—lots of fish: catfish, red snapper, even shark, plus blue crabs, various types of prawns & shrimp, hermit crabs (brilliantly orange & black), squid too. Bought starfruit (yellow & ridged so that the green end forms a star), lonyons (small brown berrylike balls with flesh like rambitans & a black pip, very fragrant, delicate), a big avocado, more mangosteens (memory fruit, those hard black or brown rinds, redstaining flesh inside, inedible, then in the centre soft white segments, delicious, containing the seeds.) Little bananas here too (pisang mas), very sweet. Plus durians & some other brown fruit about the size of Yucatan papayas. Papayas here grow in the garden (along with purple & white eggplants & orchids), are large & deep orange inside like the mameys.

Another swim this p.m., all of us in the sea this time, its muddy brown waves lifting us onto coarse shale above sand where the surf comes in. No jellyfish yet, tho Dad told us not to touch the slimy bottom further out because ikan sembilan with poison spines lurk there. Pam and I swim lengths of the pool for energy, but it's the salt of the sea revives me, or memory, some further dimension. Stood in the clubhouse after with an ayer limau (fresh limejuice & water) & watched the sea breaking on the sand & rocks below, the foamy edge of wave curling around the rock, soaking into sand as it withdraws drawing lines immediately effaced, & the long recession of the wave only to be thrown up again & again, reminded me of some, the same, watching long ago. Must get out to the lighthouse at Muka Head.

*   *   *

Today was filled with birdsong—meditating at noon it was the birds came through, their shared public space a song arena where each declares itself, insists on its presence, full of life & brilliant there with (just jumped up in fright as a black beetle ran up my skirt!)

                          . . . liquid
& metallic rings, trills, calls . . . Mr.Y. comes by in pajamas & robe,
looking for the paper. . .

Want to get this down: this morning such a beautiful awakening to
curtains of rain falling around the house off the open verandah outside
our room (which *is* the room we used to sleep in, the "nursery"—Pam
recalls running around the verandah, it's familiar to me too) & that
wet noise dense with a thicket of birdsong, jubilant, joyous, in the wet,
& the falling rain transformed into falling notes, falling & ascending,
crossing the rain in darts of melody—wooden shuttle of the Thai silk
weaver—running across & through the warp of the rain. I didn't want
to wake up but to rock there between sleep & waking in the cool, in
that liquid & musical world, so deeply familiar I was hardly present
anywhere, just to be, in that long childbeing, sentient, but only just,
skin (not even 'mine') merging with an air that is full of melody &
rain-breath, breadth, sound enwrapt—

"abandoned"

      memory, *memor*, mindful
      mer-mer-os, one
      anxious thought

grey flats signal
not cement, not broken
glass

      BUNGAH / banged up
sea, its glint
broken

        waves coming in
sand shock, rock
'd asleep in the arms of
(murmurous

      jellyfish
ikan sembilan & things
pinch in the dark
      where feet go

landmark!

road coming up
at once unknown
& plain

      as concrete

FLOWER

    's

      BEACH

crossing by

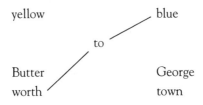

yellow   blue

          to

Butter   George
worth   town

          ferry—

Pulau Pinang Pulau Jerejek Pulau Rimau

          & the light plays
                    surface

Pulau blue distance leper
          haze, the Straits

of Malacca, your grandmother

                    silver rack for toast
                    for tennis, & the
                    gardens of night-blooming
                    kengwah
                              orchids, once
                    every five years, the place

                    "we see with alien eyes"
                    "we walk with alien feet"

lifts/

        no rickshas now but 'teksis'
& K. Tinderoomy found
in the railroad yard
his hand, his right leg severed

Butterworth a name
        "we commit
        to memory"

a life not of our own
        making

mem sahib

"mistress
of her own
house"

loved
mah mee, ordered
chicken for dinner
eased

deaths & small
wounds, cure-all,
any sepsis, except
her own

still played, gaily
mummy, mah jong, didn't
know what to "do"
(it mattered
apart from the children's
small world to move into

& lost, finally, found off-
center, *mata*, her unruly
self
unloved, locked
up in a picture, trembling
under the mask

mata hari, sun
sun through all her rooms she
closed the curtains on

planters

liquid white latex
drips   from the tree's
girdled trunk

      no, he says, no
cause of death   a
tapping, they
milk, these women in
gummy pants transporting
"even the women drive now"
churns
              down those hill
sides he climbed
refusing a guard, knows
"his people"   she
              feeds
children of the crèche
cod liver oil each morning
legs so swollen now they
climb the drive, opening
mouths like
birds
      "we'll carry on
til we can't walk
any longer"

as the buildings stand, *they*
fade into the land, unceasing
estate
      "in which the whole
      household of nature swings"

trees
they go on standing

This morning Mr. Chu from the office took the 3 of us to the Khoo Khongsi, the Khoo clan house, biggest in Penang & highly ornate, all intricately carved wood that's been gilded & the tall interior sides covered with magnificent drawings of the gods riding mythical beasts: unicorns, giant turtles with rhinoceros heads, winged panthers. The Sikh jagar watchman turned out to be also the Scout commissioner for the island. Mr. Chu is small & round & loves Johnny Cash which he plays loudly on cassette tape in his Toyota.

Yesterday we drove out to the Sungei Ara estate owned by a fine old English couple, must be in their 70's now, they've lived out here 50 years. She's a trained nurse & still administers first aid & looks after the health of the workers & their children on the estate. He speaks Malay and Tamil fluently. She probably does too as she established a day care ("crèche") for the children of Tamil workers who are mostly tappers. We watched 2 girls tapping rubber trees & later saw the liquid white latex (caught in drips from the tree by an inserted metal spout & clay cup) transported in churns to the factory where it is mixed with water & an acid that makes it congeal into long white sheets which are pressed & then smokedried, turning them amber.

Their "bungalow" a very aery open house, one whole wall of living room open to the outdoors, a lifetime of mementos & curios collected, from silver sailing trophies to a stuffed tree rat, pest on the estate as it eats into coconuts which are grown for sale, as are cocoa beans, nutmeg & cloves.

All the workers we met, in their facial expressions & manner of speaking, indicated affection & respect for him. He himself is very unassuming, they both are, & positive in outlook. When they were reminiscing about the war, we learned she'd sent her only daughter to friends up Penang Hill as the Japanese were advancing, so she could be free to scrounge up rice reserves to feed their workers who had very little food. During the postwar emergency period when communist guerillas were setting up road ambushes & taking over estates, he refused to be accompanied by a policeman in his work about the place because the policeman "walked so slowly, just plodded along, I'd never have got to the top of the hills." They relied on their own guards about the house & the loyalty of their workers. One of them reported being approached by a man who'd offered $50 for information regarding Hugh's daily activities: "he said his tuan lived in town & only came out when he felt like it so he was very sorry but he couldn't oblige the man because he didn't know." A debt they recognized.

She's a tall gangly woman with poor hearing now & badly swollen legs but when I asked her whether they had any plans for selling the estate she said oh no, they were going to carry on until they couldn't walk any longer & then somebody else would do the work for them— they had no desire to go back to England. They seem to be more in touch with the land & the people than anyone else we've met— perhaps it's their age that stops them from the kind of social small talk of the others, a curious jaded brilliancy that seems quite rootless. She especially is silent, probably because of her hearing, but they both seem to fade into their land. It's a humanly dense world too, with its Malay kampong & mosque, Tamil housing, & Chinese stores forming a small village most of the buildings of which he himself has kept up or had rebuilt. They don't seem to close off from any of it, a kind of empathy that would probably make them vulnerable if they weren't British to begin with & committed to a paternalistic system (she still administers cod liver oil daily to all the day care kids who must walk up to the house to get it now she has difficulty getting around). They really do represent the moral best of the old system—what Mrs. Khoo complained of missing when she said the Chinese long for "the good old days of the colonial system where there was real democracy & the fittest man won, regardless of race." Which no doubt reflects more on the difficulties of Malay nationalism than the virtues of the caste system of British colonialism.

*   *   *

Palms so far: betel palm (the tree of Penang, sez Hugh), coconut palm (coconuts here are green), atap palm (they use for thatching roofs), oil palm (whole plantations of), toddy palm (toddy from flowers). & hands, palms—of the man sliding down the tree so fast, who with one blow of his machete offered us a drink—sweet, slurped from inside glistening walls, split to the light, of coconut well.

July 28th

Dear Cille,

. . . It's not so much a holiday as a curious psychic re-dipping in the old font, & most of the time I'm kicking against it. Because it's so insidious, the English habits of speech & perception, English patterns of behaviour. (Suppose I got the longest conditioning anyhow, of the 3 of us kids.) But what's amazing is that it still exists, much as it has done, tho obviously it's the end of an era. It ain't my era, or Pam's, tho everyone we meet seems to want to suggest it is, implicate us in it. I've never before understood what a big move it was for them, to come to Canada.

Sometimes I panic—I want to rush home, as if I might get trapped here, this honeyed land. Mrs. J. saying how she didn't want to leave Penang, "it's such a beautiful place." It is, & yet it all feels unreal to me—there's no authentic ground here for "Europeans." I want to rip out of myself all the colonialisms, the taint of colonial sets of mind. That's why as kids we hated everything "English"—not because it was English but because we equated what was English with a colonialist attitude, that defensive set against what immediately surrounds as real on its own terms—because to take it on as real would mean to "go native" & that was unthinkable to them.

July 29th

Dad speculates, as we peer over the bridge into the rushing darkness of the brook, cicadas trilling all around us, that in some previous life he must have been a rich Chinese in Malacca with a fleet of junks trading spices to China. Says he always feels at home here, loves the smell of camphorwood chests, the songs of birds, the plants. I ask him has he never felt alien, never felt there were places he couldn't enter, wasn't welcome in? He says only recently, with the political situation the way it is, but that before, the only animosity he remembers encountering was in the Indian temple where he filmed the Typoosum rites & he could understand that. That leads to the further comment that he's never liked Indian temples anyhow.

What we make our own—or separate from us. The interests of the Chinese middle class here as commercial as the British, & the same sense of formality, & pragmatism.

Earlier, as we rode a trisha down to the Chartered Bank Chambers, Pam wondered how people on the street regard white women (she herself thinks English women look "dumpy") & whether they found us sexual or not, commented on the looks various people gave us as we passed. We both felt separate & visible in our hired trisha pedalled by someone else (an incredibly skinny man)—uncomfortable parodies of the leisured class. Is this the only way to be a white woman here? Or is this the condition of being a member of an exploitive & foreign moneyed class?

& yet the sun shines on all of us alike—everywhere the flare of colour, glint of metallic thread running thru a sari, shining flesh, oil gleaming off black hair—we feel pale by comparison, & immaterial (living always in our heads?) It's the same feeling I had coming home from Mexico, that people walk the streets of Vancouver mostly as if they are invisible. Here people sleep on the sidewalks, piss in the gutters, women nurse their babies by the roadside, everyone selling food & eating it, or fingering goods, or eyeing each other (likewise tactile)—but not separate. The press in the streets is almost amniotic, it contains & carries everyone.

Today I've heard both an Indian (the cloth salesman in the market whose son is training to be a doctor in England) & a Chinese (Catholic convert, committed to both Christianity & the English language,

living in a nation devoted to advancing Islam & teaching Malay)
protest against the unfairness of the Malayanization policy of the govt
(e.g. how 65% of all university entrants must be Malays, the other
races compete for what's left). & yet this *is* Malaysia & the largely rural
& labouring Malays have a lot to catch up on, fast. I can't believe the
the stereotype passed on to us that they're "lazy," don't want to work,
don't have a head for business, etc. & yet how long, how many genera-
tions these Chinese & Indian families have lived here, feel they
belong, & then are separated off on the basis of race. All the separa-
tions.

vs. Canadian 20's

bahasa malaysia

sungai, bukit, tanjung
river, hill, cape

> "sometimes i panic
> i want to rush home
> as if i might get
> trapped here"

pulau cantik
this beautiful island only
the coarsest of maps
show
      jalan jalan, roads
to the heart of
      (Ayer Itam, black
      water

*"all
people know that
the sea is deep"*

      red backers
      bad hats

*"I have not read the
newspapers yet"*

i see
flame trees rain
trees still flower
unnamed, out of that earth

      bumiputra
      sons of,
        inhabit

hujan, angin, ribut
rain, wind, storm
clouds are gathering

& the sacred island of Potoloka
Throne of Kuan Yin in
the China Sea of

    T. Poh's Guidebook
      to the
    Temple of Paradise

is not, is overlaid
like Paradise itself
on this place

   "Dang, dang, kong
   Kuching dalam tong…"

"Raju also likes to read fictions"

& pulling
the cat out of
the well

   name
what feet dig into
each day's sewage
& all that shit
   inter-
national finance
leaves

   a trail
under the trees
   (*pokok pokok*

     say, "Jalan Peel"

Penang
July 23/76

Love,

Frangipani fading on the desk, Eng Kim just ran by in bare feet, so quiet in pajamas, it's 6 p.m., post-tea, post evening rain like a monsoon, mosquitoes out in the fading light (dark here by 7) & what i've tracked in the birdbook as the black-naped oriole (a yellow as brilliant as the saffron robes of the yellow men monks) trilling from the trees, flame of the forest just outside my window. . .

(dusky pink cheecha playing peekaboo behind a gilt frame, me not at all sure i want to feel those pale pink lizard feet suddenly land here, just shot up the wall to nab a midge then leap six inches onto a post & disappear to a ledge four feet above me) so much life here not even the walls are still . . .

It's strange being a princess again, the sheer luxury of this house, its spaciousness, its accoutrements (every bedroom has its own bathroom), everything kept spacious, uncluttered, unlittered & clean by servants who pick up after you, wash your clothes, cook your food, do your dishes, ad nauseum (a little work would make me feel at home). & Eng Kim herself, oh Roy that is the strangest. I recognized her as soon as she came down the steps to greet us (old baronial family style), she's hardly changed in 25 years, still climbs the stairs with all that girlish quickness & like any good servant, utterly silent. But more her smile— it's as if i'd never gone away i know that smile so completely & love it, yes it's the love that astonishes me. That face told me as much as my mother's, by its changing weather, how the world was with me, or against, what i, as any rebellious child, was up against. I must have spent hours of accumulated moments watching it. & yet her face is not maternal in any way, at age 45 or whatever it's still utterly girlish & in our smiles i catch a little of the old mischief we shared, playing our own peekaboo with all the rules.

& my god, the rules of the house & how it's been explained to Pam & me several times that we mustn't "upset the routine," how difficult it is to finally "get things done the way you want them" (breakfast at such & such an hour, for instance, & how the toast or coffee should be etc.),—how "they" get confused if you alter things, so that the routine becomes itself a prison. As the women of the house, Pam & I are supposed to "look after things," give the orders, make sure the system functions smoothly. Both of us dislike the role & like children, rebel by acting dumb. What we want is to break down the wall the the separates us from Eng Kim in the very fact of our roles & yet we haven't quite figured out how.

Except that tonight we began by earlier expressing an interest in the terrible durian fruit whose stench has been much mythified since we were little (& the old durian tree in the garden where our dog was buried is gone, cut down). One of the Chinese men in the office said he'd be happy to bring some durians round for us to try tonight & kindly did so. Mr. Y., when told, requested that they not be brought into the house (haven't i learned the dialect well?) so our benefactor & Pam & I regaled ourselves at an old wooden table on the walkway from kitchen to servants quarters, as he chopped them open with a cleaver (they look like wooden pineapple bombs) & split the meat to reveal the butterycovered seeds: an incredible flavour, not fruitlike, something like coffee & bitter spices compounded with onions, really strong. Eng Kim & Ah Yow (the cook) love them & when we brought Dad down to try some a little while later, they were perched on the table happily eating away & watched with amusement Dad's valiant but obviously ginger chewing & swallowing—Eng Kim's amusement in her eyes tho she'd never speak it to "the tuan."

I'm going to stop this, being haunted by echoes of earlier (age 12 etc) letters & journals, that so stilted proper English. "To the manner born." How completely i learned to talk Canadian (how badly i wanted to). & how fast it drops away here. Wonder how it sounds to you?

July 25th

Sunday & the frangipani blossoms on the desk have gone all brown.
Hot today, hottest yet, tho it clouded over as usual (haven't seen a
sunset, been mostly cool for here, & cloudy—waterfalls of rain the
other morning, woke up to its wet descent all round the open veran-
dahs of the house, the open windows—no glass on some, for breeze).

We drove up to Ayer Itam, the Buddhist hill shrine—driving is such a
trip. I love winding thru throngs of brilliant sarong & sari dressed
women, children, sellers of ramibitans & chinese noodles, cyclists of all
sorts, young chinese youths zooming by on Honda bikes, cars trucks
hundreds of buses all dodging the cyclists & the goats. Went up to the
reservoir above the temple & walked a path thru jungle, o the smell
came back so vivid, that deep sandloam fern palm dank smell. Everybody drives on the left here so the whole car is reversed, i keep reaching for an invisible gear shift & frightening Dad & Pam by turning into
oncoming traffic. But i think i'm the only one who enjoys driving.
Unfortunately it's a fancy Ford Cortina the company owns so i can't
just take off in it whenever i want to.

My (hardwon) independence as a Western woman is being eroded
every day & of course i'm seduced by my senses into just giving in—to
the heat as much as to everything else. Finally let myself have an
afternoon nap today, but the swimming—every afternoon the sea takes
me in, old mother sea, sand dusky (no clarity like the Caribbean), &
warm.

Mostly it's a struggle, an old old resistance against the colonial empire
of the mind. For all the years that Mr. Y's been here he knows almost
nothing about what surrounds him, what the trees or birds are, what
the fruits are—he doesn't like native food, exists on a kind of dilute
European diet that includes lots of canned food. Private hedges of the
mind as complete as the locked & bolted doors, the iron schedule of
the house. Living in armed defensiveness against even the earth (don't

go barefoot, nevah, nevah, for fear of hookworm etc.) I remember it all from my childhood, the same. Everything tells me this is not where i belong (including the odd intense look from Malays, boomiputras, "sons of the soil"): the tourist experience compounded with colonial history. Europeans don't live here: they camp out in a kind of defensive splendour that's corrosive to the soul.

Aug 1st

Amah, age 74, in her sarong & shirtwaist, light gauze scarf hung round her neck, hair grey underneath the black, Amah, with her deep voice, expressive ways, "yah yah," enthusiastic confirmation when Pam turned into the right road, driving her home—home to the house she works in, still housekeeping. "Daphne mari, Pamela mari," exclaiming over & over on the fact that we'd come. A lovely resilience, living in the present, genuine affection for the "tuan," being herself a complete person with physical grace, even at 74, & dignity, not heavily insistent on it, only sufficient to herself. Her grace has to do with accepting what life brings & marvelling at it, laughing much, a deepthroated chuckle, & laying claim to nothing.

Buddhism says it is want that chains us to the world, us "hungry ghosts." & I see (just as I stands for the dominant ego in the world when you is not capitalized), that i want too much, just as, a child, i wanted affection. Growing sense of myself as a Westerner wanting, wanting—experience mostly. Anxiety arises from the discrepancy between my wants & my actual condition. Why plans so chain me— wanting too much from the day, wanting too much from others who can never be more than they are. In want : in fear. The "liberated" woman in me insisting on her freedom & in terror of its being taken away. Passive resistance a better stance. Say "yes" to restraints & simply do what you need to: act in silence.

street opera

(works, or
words & deeds

"the funniest story he told
was of going to see *Hamlet*
done as a Chinese opera"

satay

buah

mee goreng

these populous
night stalls
"already existing
web"

"action
acts into"

street
play

. .

godstick
dragon in an
old man's
sight

sharpens
all night

burnt paws
ashen ears
hear

it is 'seeing'
see

memory smoke

..

wayang a
       way in
          no
shadow play
but neon, new on
the old
         acts
"can be told as
a story . . . bios"
anyone's

       robe & drums

..

the solitary hero
in his cups
jumps up,
       challenged

       god comes, that
       audient
here
the act
enacts

here in the
din of the street
eating goes on
acting, speaking

heedless of all that
imitation

..

satay cups array
god's house fruit heaps
this full moon night

month of hungry
ghosts

"life" invites

..

offer them food who
come to devour
the real
banknotes, music, fruit

we think we consume

a fury of action they
who pass beyond
"actor & sufferer" both
relinquish & remember

..

night stalls

satay, buah
mee goreng

relics
we transform

"acting into"

Love,

How much of what we experience is made up by what we desire?! (&
all my questions become exclamations, what is! or, but for the type-
writer, a huge office Olympia, the other way around—what is?)

Questionings of the real, no quest. Tho it appears we're here for "the
month of hungry ghosts"—a month full of Chinese street operas, a
form of veneration—shrines set a little way from the casually erected
stages with money offerings, food offerings, & hundreds of joss-sticks
burning in sandbowls. What is strange, even precarious, is how this is
also real, this that i wake up to every morning, & as the day progresses
becomes so voraciously real it eats up all the other real where you &
Kit & Jan are, so that even its strangeness has disappeared. I've
recovered my own language & unusually today my own thought, & the
world outside the window, thick with foliage & birdsong, looks like an
embroidered backdrop or the painted canvas the Chinese operas use—
in a minute it will all roll up to reveal the next scene.

> If the world is real
> > The word is unreal
> If the word is real
> > The world
> Is the crevice   the dazzle   the whirlwind
> No
> The disappearances and the appearances
> > > Yes

>   . . . .

> > > (Octavio Paz, fortunately with me)

Maybe that's why the Chinese venerate snakes here, tho i was told it's
because snakes recall the ancient dragons of the sky, & dragons
perhaps like the Toltec snakemouths with the appearing or disappear-

ing heads of priests inside them, must signal a swallowing up of the real
in another real. Anyhow i didn't think you'd believe i actually held a
wriggly green viper, such muscular writhings in my hands, so Pam has
taken a photo as EVIDENCE—tho that too means nothing as i've
discovered the whole of the last roll of film & perhaps those before it
were threaded in wrong & weren't winding forward (as time is supposed to do—

well maybe that's it, the strange conjunctions of past &
present, a past that undermines the apparent newness of the present, a
present that unlocks the hidden recesses of memory or dream which
have also coloured it—& do i see what i haven't in some sense
dreamed?

Driving out to Batu Ferringhi, a beach i remember from childhood
trips (it's further round the island, & was, *then*, isolated, as likely as not
to have Malays surf fishing with their nets or selling rambitans from
bicycle carts) we found, Pam &i, big American-style hotels & even the
kampong houses become boutiques for tourists, & driving further,
looking for the beach i'd dreamed &/or the beach i remembered, saw
another quite different one & found myself saying this is it, even
knowing where the path down was—tho to the *eye* it was all new,
some other sense recognized it (some sense that has to do with loca-
tion, even direction, or something as abstract as contours of land)
despite its discrepancy from the picture i've carried in memory all these
years.

I dream of you & Kit, believing you exist as you usually do in a world i
know but can't escape to. Here a world is dreaming me as much as i am
dreaming it, a dream that's been going on too long , i want to wake
up. & at the same time learn, as usual, i want too much. My impa-
tience, my curiosity as a visitor can't consume this world because, in a
curious way, i'm part of it & must act out my role to reach its end.
Everyone we meet assumes another life for me than the one i actually
live (Lewis Carroll must have had this experience) & since i can't

escape (can't literally act on my own but am always being acted upon as this network of people from the servants to Dad's friends shape the parameters of my behaviour in the form of a hospitality as binding as any dream in the dreaming) i only act out a parody of myself, secretly reserving a part that observes, fighting lassitude induced by the heat, to jot down these odd notes retrieved from the unreal:

> i've drunk clear salty-sweet liquid from the inner well of a freshly hacked coconut;

> i've eaten fried cuttlefish & jellyfish at the Song River Cafe;

> i've swum in the murky heaving body of the sea, thousands of tiny transparent fish, ikan bilis, jumping all around my face no bigger than fleas;

> i've heard the chirruping language cheechas speak to each other, late at night, as they wriggle blackeyed over the white ceiling;

> i've been seduced by the voices of the clothsellers murmuring in my ear;

> i've smelt the woodsmoke of giant allday joss-sticks burning behind the kitchen of the Lone Pine Hotel, whose casurina trees lift & fall all day in the wind that lifts the sea;

> i've outraged a tamil woman squatting in the dirt of a banana seller's stall by pointing a camera at her, & learned something about dignity;

> i've drunk the warm foamy juice of sugar cane pressed by diesel engine under the neon light of a street-vendor's cart;

i've cut into a rubber tree, a Malay girl-tapper's hands
on mine, & watched the white blood ooze round its
girth;

i've been stopped by a stranger in the crowded
stairwell of the Chartered Bank Chambers & told he
used to drive me to school;

i've watched Chinese motor cycle youths, stoney-faced
Sikh families gracious in sari & turban; sleepy-eyed
children in pajamas; old Malay men in sarongs, & the
lovers of all nationalities watching us & evening pass
as the sea rolls in on Gurney Drive

later:
Dinner on a terrace above the swimming club, yellow crescent moon
shimmering above a rain tree, sunset trailing pinks across a rapid sky
falling into night over the sea Rat Island punctuates with its light
echoed by the other off the mainland, marks the edges of the shipping
channel, & i'm engaged in conversation with the widow of a planter, a
New Zealander who hasn't seen New Zealand for 25 years, who sleeps
alone in a big house overlooking the beach afraid that if she falls down
in the night no one will hear or care, & along with her servants & the
few remaining Europeans, as old & eccentric as she is, she lives out her
life in an alien country, drinking coffee, talking of shopping, of the way
things have changed, in this tropical heat taking her hot water bottle
to bed, waiting to die—tho in her bangles & beads & tinted hair, in
her gestures at independence (paying for her own drinks), utterly
dependent on her servants (her driver takes her everywhere), she'd
never admit it. It goes on like this. The stories, the characters. A sense
of melodrama pervades everyone's life, they keep track of everyone's
"end," & their lifestyle, their values are so unreal to me that i listen in,
fascinated by their reality to each other while my own recedes. These
are the ghosts, they offer ghost food, & if i stayed here & partook of it
long enough i'd become a ghost too, like the woman Pam tried to talk

to the other night who could only yawn.

Some of them speak of "going home," to England or anywhere, & some of them have nowhere to go. They haunt the place (a kind of addiction). Having experienced haunting, i see i've spent most of my life trying to live somewhere. Which perhaps means nothing more than being at home. Or some such notion of a public space as Hannah Arendt describes (*The Human Condition* has been my escape hatch to our world), where one's life takes place in a web of relations held *in common*. Plinius speaking of the effects of slavery so long ago, "We walk with alien feet; we see with alien eyes; we recognize & greet people with an alien memory; we live from alien labour . . . " could have been writing about the Straits Settlements, now Malaysia.

Cameron Highlands
August 5/76

You're either still in To. or back home—eating at Min's or the De-lightful, reading the *Sun* or gazing up at the blue (is it blue?) above the Coca Cola plant from your studio windows. It's strange to be living a day ahead of you, which means nothing since i'm not even in your world—i'm on the "roof of the world," 5000 ft. up, mist rising off the hills in morning sun. Here they even grow strawberries, amid the tea plantations. There are still *orang asli* (aboriginal people) who live in the jungle, wear loincloths & hunt with poisoned darts & blowguns— which all the little stores in Tanah Rata sell, along with gigantic rainbow butterflies, the largest of which is named Rajah Brooke, after the 19th C. English adventurer who ended up as Rajah of Sarawak, in perpetuity, etc., & in between the Fanta & fried mee stalls, the dusters of dyed pampas grass & piles of Cameron Highland oranges, you'll hear American rock & roll on the radios, a la Beach Boys or Everly Broth-ers, & even the humblest Tamil shacks in Bringchang sport TV antennae—everyone's been watching the Olympics in that exotic, foreign, Canadian town.

Here, here it's
    prayer fronds of
        tree ferns

           leaf hands
                i wave toward you

                    through the
                    stillness of

                          blue air

"hantu hantu"

house up the Hill not far from the Crag Hotel,
no one slept in, or fell asleep & woke in the jungle she said—
we were shown its tile roof slanting up from the trees,
licked ices on the Hotel terrace & looked, our bodies
safe on scratchy chairs, definitely there, fretting under the
straps of our sundresses, white shoes tapping toward an
acrobatic gesture off the low wall ("don't you dare") into
that green massif of leaf cloud, swaying below . . .

as a cup fills itself in the stream

undoing it, the clasp on the trunk . . . always there were voices calling
to each other in another language rising through the house, full of
incomprehensible import, intent on each other, saying something even
in the chatter . . . what was being told she was excluded from? did she
wonder? . . . is rusty & sticks, because of humidity, but pulling it open
finally there is first the smell of must, moths, all it was designed to
prevent . . . no basement there under the house, no damp concrete
shoring up earth, no sawdust bins, no furnace. but two stone steps up
off the earth & onto tile an inescapable light falls along, all those
rooms light & aery, & when the sun comes in, unrolling the chicks,
her hands on the white cord uncoiling it off the little cleat, & then the
bamboo mutter of the blind unrolling shadow . . . but not anything
dark, nowhere the sun *didn't* come, except perhaps their rooms at the
back by the dark wall of the cliff where she went slippers slapping tile
& the swish of pajamas against her legs . . .

> *"Betsy and Derek were*
making a plan to run away from the orphanage . . ."

lifting the old catch, a
little stiff, told to be careful . . . two mothers, two, but one mother &
the other someone we had a claim to, we thought of almost as part of
ourselves, her hands our hands to bathe us, dress us, & the gentle
combing of our hair, & young—did we see her? & a third who cared for
the house, Amah, had seven children "& they all died, my dears," who
cared for us too, sloppy & merry & what did it matter? except what the
Mem says. What the Mem says goes (sometimes). what the Mem says
exists as a separate entity in the house, to be listened to & walked
around, with suitable contrition if asked (giggling in the back rooms),
but separate, separate from the way life moves, on. what the Mem says
was meant to last. like mercurochrome on a cut. like the contents of a
steel trunk . . .

*"They both took out of the wardrobe all their clothes and they
counted their money which was three pounds and they put it into their
suitcases. They got dressed and packed their night clothes . . ."*

                                              lifting the
lid which was heavy, painted with the letters of her name in white,
stencilled as all the linen was inked in black along one seam, the
letters of our family name & her initials, because she was the one who
telephoned down the hill angry for lost sheets, shirts, handkerchiefs,
"they'd rob us blind!" trying to make them understand, satu, dua, tiga,
TIGA! clapping her hands, Amah! her voice and & theirs, Mem?
Mem?, swirling currents through the house, always something undone,
always looking for someone, mana ada Eng Kim? Mum! Mum! always
accident prone, tch tch, tumbang? . . . blood & mercurochrome & the
big knives on the chopping block, big vats of steam, crabs lashed to the
bamboo pole, slow moving pincers, slow white-eyed stalks turning,
boil them alive? . . . "and here comes a chopper to chop off your
head" . . .

     *"Derek went down to the kitchen and got thirty tomatoe, egg and
honey sandwiches, all the cakes a whole tin of biskuits, a tin of tea (teh) two
loaves of bread a pot of honey, a pot of jam, a block of butter, two bottles of
milk and a tin of coco . . ."*

lifting it there is first of all that smell, faintly mildewed (old shopping
papers lining the bottom, her voice on the phone ordering Cowlac,
ordering apples, *not* pisang mas, *not* rambitans), faintly mothball
(Georgetown Dispensary wormpills & carbolic acid, alcohol), faintly
the sweet (Chanel) smell of temple flowers gone brown. always both
on her hands done with the day's ministration to the vase, to snakebite, to bloody knees. & always that stillness. rushing in to find (the
dog! the chickens! my sister!) her, rapt in a bleeding fragrance of
flowers' heaped cut stalks jagged toward her, setting handfuls of soft
bloom in water . . . hers the "house of flowers," her first, rumah

bungah, named in that talk that ran, knowing incomprehensible
current from kitchen to kitchen . . . & quick angry words, impatient,
& quick! emergency (kabun drunk & beating up his wife again, the
dog run over, the child dying in the back room), the dying flowers,
scorpion & snakebite, mad monkeys screeching in the trees,
unexpected storms & penance & strange tension (always "incomprehensible") . . .

*"The lady who was the head mistress was called Mrs.
Granville. Betsy and Derek hated Mrs Granville . . . "*

against this, saving
(a life) , saving (a dress), saving a future, to be passed into our eager
hands lifting the sequined bodice, lifting the promise. army surgeon's
daughter off to the ball, thai-dancers round her wrist, floating
handpainted scarf. shantung silk, watching her be fitted, pins in
mouth, "when you grow up". . . Abbott & Costello, too fat, i'll never
look like you . . . this tender flesh, perfumed & slender, bending to
kiss, cannas & cannon & nightblooming kengwah. he waited in the
wings as she said goodnight, he in white, auburn & smelling of English
Leather . . .

*"'And we could call the stream whith the waterfall Rushing
Stream and the pond Swimming Pond,' said Betsy. So they put the tent up in
Foxglove Clearing and went to sleep on some pillos in the tent with the door
shut . . . "*

naming, trying to steep me in it, with the order of the day,
with tiffin, naptime, & while they all slept sitting up in the lounge
with the doors shut, chewing the rubber end of a revolving pencil,
transparent, shines like amber in the light, pushing lead across the
lined pages of Penang Kindergarten and Preparatory School Exercise
Book . . . past "ini, mini, minah mari" now heard faintly from upstairs
. . . past the feel of little fish nibbling at my legs when I got in the

goldfish pool with Amah hitching her sarong up around her thighs, giggling kissy kissy, fishy lips nibbling at my skin under the sundress. "we're not supposed to do this." "tida apa, tida apa" . . . lying on the bench by the summerhouse alone, feeling lips all warm, a bellyful of power so big i walked with a stick under, the witch loving me had done it, "tell-tale tit! your tongue will be slit" . . .

"'O bother. Betsy you had better stay here while I get the tools oh yes I'd forgotten I'll have to get the flannels to wash ourselves whith and our towels and swimsuits.' 'Alright,' said Betsy because (because?) she did not like the idea of staying in the woods . . ." (di-hutan)

taking them off, these false promises . . . because the order changes, o my mother who should know. wetting the stems of cut zinnias against their death, their vivid heads lighting the tile in the dark heart of the house where *she* washed the dishes, staring through a little window at us in the summerhouse, Ungimah always angry. & it was always summer for us, the only dark theirs at the back, the stifling single sleeping rooms, the deep cement washpool where water was always lapping over. but *we* had words. & the words could not command their lives, only their hands . . .

"Betsy opened the two suitcases and found her paints and paintbook and started painting, but she could not concentrate . . ."

yours could not command mine, my disorderly desire, having given my word & yet sneaking out of the house . . .

"At last she put her paints away and started making the beds but she could not make them . . ."

leaving the garden, climbing the terrace where jungle was, climbing guilty toward that flower . . . but you *know* you weren't supposed to be out there! . . . for you, mother, to prove. orchids do grow wild on the terrace you said no flowers would grow. reaching to pluck, when the snake, shot across it . . .

WHY DON'T YOU LISTEN? having been told, having been told so often, such an old story . . . but it was you i lost in your word, firm as your will, your body your will, in filmy dress bending to break the spell of anger finally as you leave . . . white . . . tulle . . . don't go . . . dress with the coffee-coloured beads . . . don't leave . . . embroidered silk, gold colour . . . "give me your word" . . . promise of the body i would grow into, if i listened, if i learned to stop breaking it, my word given to you, learned to keep to the house i was meant to inherit . . .

"At last she went out shutting the door of the tent as she went . . ."   *dan terbang pur . . .*

i broke my word, i broke a new & muddy ground, i did, at last i went out, shutting the lid, closing the door of your house as i went. but it was you i left. gone down with the flowers, gone down in the mad wind of your anger suppressed. how did you break? how was it broken in you? . . . "misi chukup chukup jahat" . . . bad, bad with the curl, in the middle of your for'ead . . .

"She ran out of the woods and ran behind the bushes . . .   pokok pisang, pokok pisang . . .

i will dance it out for you, when you left, turned out, turned out of the house into the traffic, yes this & no that, you going the wrong way, you stay on your side of the road, contrary, won't go along with, these proprieties. & so a crash, so wild hysteria & the signals change, erratic. lift stout brown legs, jump up & down for chaos in black satin bodice (o bother the hat) skirt a wild swirl of colour, no i *won't* play it, *won't* say it, *won't* do it your way . . . your way . . . driven down into that black river . . .

the old order breaks, mother, those garden paths, seed beds, tiny trunks all split open at last in the icy grip of anger, shine destruction, shine what spills over, shine black ice all over the heart . . . & where it bubbles up, there, there at the heart of the house a dark pool they ignored & taught you to, NOT because you thought it was wiser, but caught, caught in the old ways, there mother-daughter, i call you up through the spring of a new . . . word . seed . season . . . whole, it comes back, it fills always where you were.

this is not

this is not my world, i can't live here—lighthouse, on the far
strands i dreamt, i dealt myself a hand—this is where we were,
berthed in an alien place, light turning all around—for a while,

we were housed in it, walked *out* to it, mother, father, sisters,
over the glistening sands & the light, welled out of the sky we
waded through, it shone on us too . . .

"we were never there, we never visited a lighthouse much less stayed."

that is another world turning, o father, o ambush of the sun . . .

the line

Begin at the beginning, she thinks, there was no beginning, or only
one dimly remembered from her place at the round teak table, highly
polished, her sister sits opposite, a table so big they can't touch hands
across, the hall (it was *all* big then they were so small) stretches its
black & white tile pattern to the door, its white grille pale green plants
stare outside of, staring into the amber light where they sit, inside,
forming a square at the round table, her father to the left, their host to
the right at what is, indisputably, the head of the table, tho it is
round—he sits with his back to an electricpink screen that hides the
kitchen entrance where the servants come, softly, in bare feet over the
tile, carrying plates or removing them. & her father is not 'her' father,
he is 'their' father, tho she thinks (like any child she is the centre of
her world?) her sister looks far away, perhaps because she is not eating
(eat up, she is told, eat up, tho that is not the word, not 'up' with 'eat,'
that is Canadian, that is something they never said, her parents, tho
now their grandchildren are spoken to in exactly those words), she sits,
like a little girl in her short smock, this woman who has two children,
little, her younger sister, middle, she sits in the middle of her own field
of vision with her back to the door, & beyond her stretches the long
hall—she remembers it dark under the stairs on her way to the door,
she goes back, she remembers two bottom steps which are, inexplicably, stone after the flight of polished wood leading up, she used to sit,
waiting for them to be ready, she used to sit with her feet on the
black&white chequered tile, did she jump, from black to black? did she
spend a long time waiting? at the bottom step, stone like those outside,
& she wanted to go outside, into the world)

Are you sure you won't? he
is asking, their host, he is passing the silver basket of toast to her to
pass on to their father, this table so large they must pass from one to
the other, & tho it is bare in front of her sister, as she requested (did
she come down so as not to leave a hole in the passing?) he asks again,
you won't? you absolutely won't? with that imperceptible shake of his

head that is not a shake but, after all these years amid the doings of inexplicable people, a deploring & assenting nod, as much as to say, look here, she won't, she absolutely won't. & they look at her sister, they all do look at her resolute smile that glints under its grown politeness, glints with five year old implacability, even rebellion, she won't, she absolutely won't. It's the heat, he sighs, passing the salt he always passes, will you? take some? take lots of salt, & turning again, you must keep up your strength you know. She doesn't respond & her father assumes his usual role, there at the other end of the table, facing their host he explains, well you know we've all had so much to eat since we arrived that she feels she's been overdoing it a bit. Do you? he says with surprise, do you? I'm getting too fat, she says, glorying (ah she knows that glint) in the plainness of the fact.

Really! he says again, buttering the toast so white, so thin light shines thru, as it shines onto his skin, a palour of small wrists extended out of the cuffs of the silky shirt he wears with tie, a veneer of silk & silver, of silver knives that deploy the light, shining from the chandelier off his body's pallor of years spent in the tropics, it's the manifest routine of silverware & glass setting his place, & theirs, each in deference to the others, a space rescued by light from the dark outside she nonetheless wants to go out in, & he, he wants the light uncomplicated by any irrational tremors, his 'really' only a punctuation mark as he lays his knife on the side of his plate & resumes his soup, resumes the conversation: that man, you know spends all his life at the office, i should think he sleeps there (& the plants lean in from the white porch, attentive, opening pale green fronds as his voice assumes a confidential tone in the air that wafts thick & warm from the night, from the dark she hears, dimly, the sound of gongs & a drum, & glances across the orchids to her sister who seems to be listening),well, he has three wives you know, & i suppose the going gets a bit tough at home poor thing, with a smile at her, implying, you wouldn't want to be one of three would you, i mean, is it conceivable? Three! her father exclaims, are they still doing that? Well it's cruel really, he's living far beyond his means & this year he even asked for half his provident fund.

Can he do that? their father
asks, frowning above the soup spoon poised halfway to his mouth as
mental dossiers flick, she can see them, back thru the years (she
remembers stories of stolen furniture, thieves at night, malaria—but
where did it all begin, begin, when she was so small? the line that was
drawn to protect them from the strange, to return them to a past she
feels distinctly separate from, she & her sister, implicated at their
source), o he's entitled to it of course, they all are at the age of 55 or
whatever (simply then the company they keep? these two old friends
from a remembered world, paid tribute to in the way he holds her
chair, even her father has moved back to, a code that binds & separates as the table, at its polished surface, black, reflects the movement
of their hands, these men at opposite ends who politely break their
toast while outside, outside the cicadas hum in a deafening surf that
crests) & yet (that falls) what can you do? he enquires of her, earnestly
it would seem, they don't think of the future except as something that
arrives in the end you know, without their lifting a hand so to speak—
even her smile complies, complicit in its understanding. No she *doesn't*
understand, why is she part of this? except that she is here, her bare
feet she is not supposed to have (hookworm, my dear, he said, you
must wear slippers) flat on the tile, its black&white squares leading off
where her eyes will go, over her sister's hair, her face averted, listening
(is she? or dreaming of bed, bored) secretly feeling the tile that is cool,
cool to her feet & worn, real. Or is that the temple of this afternoon
they must take their shoes off in (& she wondered, maliciously, what
he thought of hookworm *then*—unholy thoughts, she took it seriously,
the tile those hundreds of feet were treading along with hers, no
different, no other than, worn soles on the lotus buds their guide
remarked, you too, like the buddha, dozens of buddhas, & if you pray to
this one you will receive prosperity, to this good luck, to this good
health, & each of them with alms slots)—well it's a gamble really, isn't
it, as to which expires first, the fund or his years, & who knows what
might happen, i mean they *think* this way, maybe he'll shave his head

& put on yellow robes like his brother—his brother?—a director of the company mind you, just two weeks ago. Her father leans back in his chair & roars, his laugh like a thunderclap against the ultimate absurdity of things, while their host nods, that wink, that deploring shake of his head that affirms, he did, he did, tho he says, it's disgraceful really, we can't have monks running the company can we? Her sister grins, across the orchids she sees it, a grin that echoes pure delight in the breakdown of order (imp, at the edge of the terrace dancing, grinning, who long ago threw all the house keys into the jungle, Eng Kim's, from the corner of her eye she sees her hover behind the electricpink screen, dart forward in bare feet & black pants flapping at the ankles, trying to see, have they done with the soup, & should she signal, as acting Mem is there some sign she should give, as their absent hostess, as her absent mother would have done—a confusion of flowers, of roles, Eng Kim's i am so sorry (their being here instead of their mother?), & she knew the regret was real, felt, herself, a childish confusion of Eng Kim & mother extant, her sister, eyeing the orchids where did mom learn to arrange flowers, these look so much like hers, & their father, sharp, it was your mother who taught Eng Kim, saying now, you see what an extraordinary country this is (& with that comment, clean, he separates what she wants to enter, asking how it enters her, her life which began its dim beginnings here).

Look at the mess that other one's got himself in, he says, so easy, beginning another story (& do beginnings inevitably shape what follows?), checked as she enters, who seems to fade away as soon as she leaves the screen, fade into the tile she treads, smile eclipsed in a small salute that says, excuse me, please carry on, while the hands that used to dress her deftly remove their soup bowls. *There* is a beginning, surely, a lost place, a dimly remembered space at the back of the house where the servants live & which they tiptoed round last night, whispering, two small children, i think she's disappointed in us, wondering why they couldn't pass thru polished surfaces of wood, of tile, to the dull-lit innards of the house, each with their own guilts, she remembers how i threw her keys away, she thinks i still want my own way. failing to bridge the divide a tileroofed corridor covers, a place to hover where the washing hangs, hand done, & every afternoon in the heat of the day that heavy iron, must be antique, she said, failing to ask the right questions, wanting to ask, what was it like for you? who evades, it is not customary, or that was her private beginning, an English family. & with the English how custom persists: 'as Mary's away will you please look after the meals, give the orders.' who used to look after *them* & now, with her English English, acts as translator for the other, Ah Yow, who stands firmly on her flat feet a chuckle & a shrug, well what's to be done? The meals look after themselves they found, fridge door opening to reveal what was already frozen inside, each day of the week, now thrust before them, Ah Yow frowning down at the work of her hands, pork chops & roast potatoes ('she doesn't like to cook you know, but really she's quite good'), followed by Eng Kim with two bowls, o it looks like okra, & her father, what's okra? o i remember these (& the brinjals, baskets of, eggplant piled by the roadside, white eggplant growing by the stream), Eng Kim, he persists what do we call these? ladies' fingers, she informs, with her delicate English accent. 'We,' what a strange fabrication & yet, leaning over the stone bridge into the rushing darkness of the, 'brook' they called it, that muddy ditch, coming back was coming home he'd said, in some previous life i must have been a rich Chinese in Malacca with a fleet of junks trading spices to China, & she'd disbelieved his possession of the place. Glancing over, she sees him chasing the ladies' fingers with a silver fork & spoon, as Eng Kim lowers the bowl a little for him, she sees, in the very thrust of his neck, in the frown of concentration, impatient sigh that evokes her concern, Eng Kim's, who would do it for him, she sees the Tuan, father, head of the household she inhabited as a little girl waiting, one foot on the white square, one foot on the black, in her white socks & shoes, waiting for them all to be ready, Daddy was taking them out.

What she wanted was outside, on streets she wasn't allowed to walk or ride down, on her new bike, wobbly & nervous into a world the sound of a gong invokes even now, in the

receding splash of cricket hum, treefrogs, the same frenzy to be out,
where she imagines the lights are & the people, a fury of ghosts, of
drums, a world as foreign as the streets they have no map to (he, you'd
think the government would at least provide the tourists with something, & someone else had said, but they don't want any accurate maps
released because of the terrorists, as if the terrorists didn't already live
there, bribes & threats, 'red backers,' they said, 'businessmen confess
their part in giving aid.') That was today's story & it was somebody's
version, & somebody else's naming as real, as the plate she now looks
down on, somebody else will disbelieve, as she, if she looks up, will
disbelieve his earnestness as he always says, their host, always the last
to be served, will wave his hand in the air & entreat them, please, do
carry on, as if it were something new they couldn't wait to set their
teeth to. Nothing has changed, there lie the same roast potatoes, the
same pork chop, same carrots & okra her mother would have served,
the chop cut up in pieces for them by amah in the kitchen, carefully
cut up & soaked in gravy—a world contained on her plate. She glances
at her sister who is looking at her plate with an amused smile, & in the
arc their eyes extend to each other, an imaginary string of little stalls,
mah mee, satay, poh peah, lit up at night by kerosene lamp & steam-
ing, delicious smells, appetites of a crowd those operatic stories play to,
living & dead, her eyes point their way to . . . take *away my wisdom &*
my categories . . .

      O look, her sister cries, just at the moment she
becomes aware of, a motion, a beating of wings coming in from the
space behind their father—bat? or moth? its too big furry body beating
in blind necessity against the ceiling, walls, they all sit up to watch its
staggering progress toward their host who rises, as if to hold the chair
for someone's entry: good heavens, it's only a moth. But its body's so
huge, she says, & they agree, watching the swollen thorax & dark
wings settle, finally, rest, like some breathless flag atop a white fluted
candle. Well you see, he bends to pick up his serviette & sits down
again, we have these creatures, smiles, with a wave of his hand at their
plates, please do carry on.

Coming in late, it wasn't the frogs plopping out of the way of the car's
tires on the curving drive, entry to the house, her sister said (she'd
come to expect it, ten seconds after the hedge), slow down, those
frogs—, or even the air that still surprised them when they stepped out
into its warmth, heavy as hands about them crossing the unlit lawn.
Their host had gone to bed & even the servants' quarters shone barely
a light, wan & faraway piercing the airless air that surrounded the
house & them, like thieves come in the dead of night to unlock, yes,
they had the key, unthieflike, the white grille door, guard door, unbolt
it top & bottom, ssh, don't wake them, grinding of iron on tile, to stick
the key in the lock of the inner door, unbolt that too, & thus, letting
themselves in, bolting & locking up, leave the key in the brass bowl on
the table—it wasn't that, but the polished wood reminded her, expanse
of black&white to the chairs, futile & bleak now, dining room with its
air of unspoken civility, it was the black polish of the table reminded
her: let's look at the moth.

       & when they switched on the light, at first
the white candle masked any penetrating glance, but there it was, still
hanging there, close up near the wick, a moulted, furry, furtive brown,
legs oddly precise, oddly tenacious in their grip on the wax where, in
spirals, suddenly they both could see, look, a mass of eggs, must be
dozens of them, o easily, almost a hundred, laid in & on & over but
generally conforming to the upward spiral of the stick. That's why she's
so huge, her sister says, leaning forward eagerly, caught in the grip of
the moth's urge, o look where they come out. They both watch the
white globule forming at the tip of the appendage that slowly tenses,
squeezes, dropping it precisely next in line to its sisters. What a strange
place to leave her eggs, she says, a candle! thinking of the giant joss-
sticks burning by the opera stage, & the shrine with its dozens of
smaller joss-sticks lit & waved by handfuls toward the deity who
loomed there, who unlocked the gates of the underworld in the month
of hungry ghosts, they said, looming over all those cups of sauce, those
piles of fruit, those offerings. & it wasn't the notion of hunger that

prompted her, but the simplicity with which those sticks were offered, smoking as they were to some unknown, to some invisible circumstance having to do with return. We should light one to *her*, she'd said tentatively. She'd like that, her sister agreed, & she knew, delighting in the unexpectedness of that homage, it was an escape from their world they wanted to offer up, & they stood there torn by difference, knowing themselves as strangers having no right.

But she couldn't have chosen a better place, her sister said, still bent forward, you can hardly see them. I was thinking of burning, she says, she thinks, does she say? this moth, the light that could be lit, a burning of white wax, white eggs. But look! & when she bends forward she sees them too, tiny grey specks, beginning caterpillars.

coming in, who

used to live here, used to
the sweep of kabun's broom
edge of a tideline morning used
to run her energy along, alone
exulting in birdsong, liquid
trills, squawks

            the long
reversible arc of his arm
swept up grass, not up, around
a kind of sortilege, kabun
at the bottom of the garden, not
looking up at the under
side of sky, in the easy
sweep of his arm, the long
advance of noon, a tide

poured through his broom
she ran, through crests of song
wave on wave, recede, while the broom
continues its faroff rush, like surf
coming in, she's gone

getting here

it wasn't you was it? you not here, underlining *To-morrow*, yourself
interlinear. In 1935 he gave you Shelley you took to Malacca, & what
i thought was "missing you" was "wishing you" a happy birthday, i not
even born, not even thought of as you used to say. he spelled Edrys
with an extra s, your brother, adding the kisses, dark x's after his name
underlined, insistent, covering distance to get to you

> *We look before and after,*
> *And pine for what is not*

                                     in tropic afternoons, with a
Welsh mountain for a name, you underlining loss or other nights
differently spelled, eyes under older skies. & even the mountain named
for some other mind Shelley knew "Shelley" was writing to, *Children of
a sunnier star, /Spirits from beyond the moon*, unearthly in white (roses
against their thorns), tennis racquet in hand exercising a lunar pull,
closed lids & heavy lidded eyes of Shelley amid tin talk, gin-&-tonic
talk of the market, sexual too, & surreal in the eyes of a wit no one saw
in you

> *Our sincerest laughter*
> *With some pain is fraught*

                                     your mirror caught a glimpse
of that place i hid, country of origin, clouding it over with lipstick &
powder, making mouths at the face going out to be addressed, assessed
by dress & manners you saw thru—you, caught out in a language that
sounded strange, stranger yourself, deprived of words that spoke what
you knew

        "they want my life"—always a life for a life, yours for ours.
sacrifice you knew they exacted. pruning of the rose, a kind of tax on
being, familial. at what cost, we couldn't hear the words for. erased, &

"*In thy place———*"

"life's cheat," deprived of any truth, as
you, long in tooth & unnamed, recede from imagination: one cloud of
thought, one word of no earthly use, "mother"—

you knew the dark,
conspiracy, how they keep power in their hands, unnamed (you forgot,
we give ourselves up to). you taught me fear but not how to fight. you,
mispelled, gave yourself to the dark of some other light, leaving me
here with the words, with fear, love, & a need to keep speaking

"*—the thing we fled—To-day*"

HOW HUG
A STONE

for Edrys who was also Tino

"you'll cross to England & you *will* walk in
'England's green and pleasant land' & she'll go home
with you, though she has been already."

Vancouver, 1975

HOW HUG A STONE

1. Crossing-over

June 14, we fly to England, landing the next day

June 15, Gatwick—train to Reading—rowhouse drizzle, laundry in the half-sun, endless brick enduring unchanged

melodic repeats of English, speech patterns volleying back & forth 2 seats away—we can't catch all of it

at Reading, my step-mother's house, this polite stranger my newly-acquired step-brother, says we met 30 years ago—over a wheelbarrow & childhood territory i vaguely remember

June 16, Kit up in the English dawn with a dream of costumes (manners) & not "fitting in"

departure

an elderly man sitting at the back says we have just left land, Baffin Island he means, now all is ice floes on black water, crazy paving they have pulled the blinds on. for the movie begins. Agatha Christie version of what we fly to, dense with intrigue. take intrigued attention to a star system elderly English lady plots, enraged mother at the heart of it: lost.

so as not to be lost, invent: one clear act in all that jazz. (in-flight—& if the plane goes down?)

invent (how we get here) flying along a sunset's brilliant flush, intricate music in one ear to dull the engine roar, its possible heartbeat stop, inventing still (to keep us aloft) a place to land at the end of all this to, . . . his blue joggers on the seat beside me, feet gone. elsewhere are we? (even here.) as he slides back in:

"i LOVE to go into that lab'ratory." "what?" "the one that has a big hunk of shit that won't go down."

thus revised, flying along a sunset with our shit, leftovers, earthladen sacs, thanks to 23,000 gallons of fossil fuel sustained aloft for a few hours improbably in a DC 10. we feed ourselves stories to dull our sense of the absurd. fed a line so as not to imagine the end—linear version of our lives unravelling in a look, back. mystery appeals to our belief that things do make sense, this plot we're in, wrapped up like knife fork & spoon.

& yet, left open, flapping, wide to the wind, without narrative how can we see where we're going? or that— for long moments now, we happen.

by train to Reading

it is the rackety clacking of the wheels that is familiar, or this sideways
motion, this compartment speeding down the line, of brick houses,
rows of washing, embankment flowers, it's my son discovering the
window open, staring head out into wind, ecstatic, until the cinder bit
in eye:

didn't i tell you?

    that was it, my vision smeared with soot like some kind of powdered
ink my mother's handkerchief a scalding rubdown, tearful eyes to the
horizon line of the cut, those fences other kids were climbing free as
they went in their unscripted world . . .

grounded in the family

ground still rushes away from me though my step-brother has named
every flower in all four directions contained by a brick wall. my host.
reading the light of Reading read in pink petals overblown. overgrown.
i am the child with chocolate smeared across her face. three frocks in a
green wheelbarrow merely photographic the way he hauls us up in
thirty years. i am the one who pushed. & she to whom we were hostage
then, hostess & mother (his): o they are all right really. wild colonials
roaring around her garden climbing walls (what else are they for?)
skinned knees. shelter from the storm, of eyes & winds & tongue
wagging, tongue lashing. badly behaved. under their, see those trees?
the weather has not been kind really. pouring tea.

under the moon a grown man now lures *moththe, math-*, worm. with a
white sheet spread on the lawn, with a bedroom lamp he lures their
bodies, heavy, beating against the walls. he wants to fix them in their
families, he wants them wing-pulled-open, pinned on a piece of
cotton, mortified. as then, i protest this play as death—despite his
barrage of scientific names, his calling to my son, you game? as if he
held the script everyone wants to be in, except the moths.

i thought i was free, turning, wild at the bottom of the garden where
the lady lies. stone white she hears our steps, faint brouhaha on the
winds of the years, turbulent turning wing flutter, worm twist, back in
our hands the beginning we took for the end. she is serene. she sees us,
ghos-ti-, not ghostly nor free—reciprocally obliged. host & guest fixed
in the one script, the prescribed line of relationship.

my son turns from me into the light of names & pins & white flutter,
captive of the play. even as i remember pushing past my mother's quick
restraint.

they were on leave in '48 with three small children, or we were. they were on leave & we were along, in a car that smelled of tobacco & leather, soft, like sitting on gloves, grey Morris maybe. inside our moveable & too-close room, the aftermath of a rebuke, watching the flasher lift its signal colour for me alone in the dark out there, to go, beyond my father's back erect & in control, my mother's body soft & angry in its hum, & warm, walls that hold, to go back, but the wheels go on, in the dark of the dials & gears & the hum.

narrative continuity

this house is familiar, a house of relics: old armoires full of kept clothes, old photographs & habits from a family life that was.

my step-brother lives in his room & the kitchen habitual in its smell of bacon, struck matches & javel. a place for everything: blueing for bee stings. tea cosy. plowman's pickle, its fruity vinegar smell when he lifts the lid recalls me to grandmother meals some thirty years ago.

relics i recognize, even family phrases i've heard from his mother in Canada. crossings-over. as my childhood family had its language, covert because "so English" in North Van. & my mother driven wild: why can't they teach you how to speak? when i brought the colloquial home, flaunting *real fine* with *me'n her*.

what was familiar now is relic: *sweetshop, pillarbox.* clipped monosylla- bles with a distinctive pitch pattern. remnants of Old English, even *moth, snake, stone.* word henge to plot us in the current flow. without narrative how can we see where we've been? or, unable to leave it altogether, what we come from?

Prospect Park

walking under them, great spreading limes in the park last night
(linden? i ask, lime he says, genus *Tilia*) but i smell the fragrance
reminds me of linden my grandmother used to mail over, tinfoil cubes
with a picture, bath salts for each of us & mine was linden a tree, or
was it the flower? not the flower he says but a sticky secretion insects
leave & he shows me the heart-shaped leaf, shiny under moonlight,
feel, stickiness dropping through the sweet night air, it's a nuisance
really, it's not what you think.

2. These Still-Standing Walls of Home

June 16, sitting on a baggage waggon outside Exeter Station—
will i recognize my aunt? my cousin i have never seen?

"looking so vile," "a fearful row"

my uncle changeable as the weather—my mother's brother for sure—
minotaur at the heart of the family maze

June 17, Poltimore village, evening—warm, silent, fragrant with hay &
silage, timothy grass (June the worst month for pollen count)

June 21, my grandmother giving back my early self to me in photographs she
foresees drained of meaning in strangers' hands

magpie augury

one for sorrow
two for joy
three for a girl
four for a boy
five for silver
six for gold
seven for a story yet to be told

never heard the magpie rhyme? incredulous, my aunt recites it, fast, as we speed down high-hedged lanes in time for tea & my uncle's arrival from his doctor's schedule, home to greet us foreign members of his family.

magpies in a field, she & my cousin tell me, tell you what to expect. their long tails, their flashy black-&-white wings. how many did you see?

& i'm intrigued, writing it down. odd-numbered *sorrow, girl, silver* (only silver) & yet, she is the one with the untold story. you hardly ever see seven, my aunt admits. as i listen to the words that tell it.

at Cogswells ("*whose* wells?")

the feel of this cottage full of dogs, cats, flowers, currents of emotion.
the drama of English manners. "sorry, darling." scones with Devonshire
cream & strawberry jam for tea. "o bloody hell, there goes the phone."
a constant stream of speech, my aunt in alliance with her teenage girls,
the jokes, the stories—"that old bag," "what rubbish," "a perfectly
horrid little house." the comings and goings of my uncle, pater familias,
Mephistophelian brows (my grandfather) with the full feminine mouth
i see in my sister, the moods of my mother, charming & furious at
once.

my son imitates an English accent, intrigued (to be in the swim) & yet
stuffed up, finding it hard to breathe. allergic to the nearest thing we
have to a hereditary home.

June near the river Clyst, Clust, clear.
Clystmois this holding wet & clear.

it's haysel, haymaking time, "Sweet an' dry an' green as't should be, An
full o'seed an' Jeune flowers." tedding & cocking going on, shaking,
turning, spreading. haytrucks go lorries lumbering by these twisty lanes
lined high with hedgerow, no seeing over, cow parsley, stinging nettles,
campion, "day's eyes" & snails all colours coiled in their leaf byways.
jeune the young, green June delayed by rain. June why do you punish
me? "Take heede to the weather, the wind, and the skie." indeed, make
hay while the sun shines you write, while the moon is on the wane. he
wanes, my son redeyed & watery, phlegmatic in the face of *phleum
pratense* grass of the meadow, timothy spikes erect a masculine given
name, god honouring. not her who is cut, full of young vigour, from the
living book, from the play of light & shadow, nothing less than herb-
of-grace, rue i find, there with the queen's pinks in the clock that is a
garden.

under Poltimore or Clystmois
("some confusion about the name"):

the red dirt of Devon, my cousin tells me, is sandstone parent material risen from the sea. parent, to get, beget, give birth. *parcae*, the Fates, who allot what you get.

whole lot of spinning & cutting going on. my aunt's wheel stands in the family room. she shows me the spindle, she shows me the distaff & tow. opening paper on a newly shorn fleece, she warns me it's the real thing, smelly she says. lanolin mixed with the dirt of Devon fields, sheep turd & grass smell, lingers on our hands all day.

what is parent material? how long do we need it? feet on the red dirt of Devon bedrock we go back to the familiar: my mother's trace, these family pathways to negotiate, these still-standing walls of home.

Poltimore, Pwyll Ti Mawr,
Pool by the Great House

smell of coalsmoke in this house. *i must warn you, it's the original grotty cotty*, actually two, Cogswells in front with the roses, Churchview in back. two parlours, two staircases, two corner cupboards to match the straight-back chairs. this plowman's hovel he calls it, 17th century brick & cob, cowdung we live among, clay, straw & pebbles these walls, two foot deep sills where winds from the southeast blow. & against that cold set a native knowing, savvy, what to do. a doctor's wife she knew this was the right place for them—her choice he can't abide. in what remains of Lord Poltimore's holdings keeping the telly company watching *A Town Called Alice*. war runs through all of our lives. "when you were born," my grandmother recalls, "& not with a silver spoon."

what is this smell of coal? damp, & so familiar. *familia*. household servants. my aunt wipes her hair from her eyes with the back of her hand covered with soot. coal stove where the family eats, where the new pup sleeps, black Blossom innocent of work & growling, grip on Dillon's ear, for fun. she hangs on.

& the bullterrier i grew up with, named after a king at the end of the war we could go back—my mother boarding ship for Penang with three small children, & the Australian nanny don't forget, & two bull terrier pups. like her mother before her, "brought up in luxury with servants & comforts of every sort. When I see what people are going through now I think how lucky I was to be born when I was." sitting straight in the room where the tv is, my grandmother imperious, "knocking up ninety," elides time, recalls at will those days, war, "we didn't know *what* was going to happen." she lights what preceded me in a voice like coalsmoke, takes me back, like smoke in the lungs it catches.

"We took your mother out at eighteen you know, in the first bloom of youth, lovely complexion. And there was a big wedding on—one of the magistrates who was marrying a planter's daughter. This wedding was held on the grounds of the Residency in Malacca, and we of course had an invitation, so that was Edrys' first public function. And, my *dear*, the Resident's daughter was very pretty, very nice, but everybody said Edrys capped it all."

& underneath, that dark vein in her voice, that music, is it Welsh? i ask her son, my son whooping it up in the background, C-3PO version of British butler tones, *my dear, she speaks like all colonials deprived of an English education. it's what we call Anglo-Indian*—singsong he means. not that play of bella-donna, music of futility i hear, atropine, compressed into fine crystal memories, unchanging, clear.

"Do you know what she wore? I can see her *now*—a lovely pale coffee-coloured organdy dress, 'twas long, shaped to the waist, rather full flared skirt & *enormous* puff sleeves. And when we were in France I bought her a huge Tuscany straw hat the same colour as this organdy dress, and I bought masses of velvet nasturtiums from the palest of yellow to the deepest of that ruby red—velvet, you can imagine how rich they were. I had bunches of these flowers on this great big hat which flopped with their weight, and a big posy of them across the front of the dress—it was lownecked of course, being in the tropics we didn't wear high collars very much—and she looked a *dream*."

her dream, the one my mother inherited, *her* dress, my mother lending her body to it. as i refused, on a new continent suffocated in changing rooms thick with resentment: you don't understand, *everybody* wears jeans here & i *want* a job. refusing the dream its continuity in what i thought was no man's land (not Rupert's, not the King's), just the trees.' topped, felled, sawn into sawdust all up & down the coast, not coal but sawdust, woodchips, whole rounds burning in the stove.

& no coals in the skep, my aunt rattles the door of the stove, removing familial ash with wry intent, Blossom at her heels. my grandmother monolithic in mauve, composed, continuing:

"We went to Penang and she said, 'Mother, I'm so *tired* of this life, of just wasting my time going out dancing every night, getting engaged to play tennis, somebody ringing up and wanting to take me out to golf. It seems so futile. I want to learn dress designing and dressmaking. I've seen advertisements and I've written off to England. I won't be coming back with you when we go on leave.' This was when we were in the hotel in Penang sitting on the grounds facing the sea just where her wedding photograph was taken a few months later. Isn't it extraordinary?"

& so coal lights, *geulo-*, ember from India born "somewhere in the north" in the 1890s, schooled in the hills, has a daughter born in Bombay, schooled in the Nilgiri Hills ("like the English downs," she said) & England, carried all the way to Malaya, thence to Australia when war breaks out, where i appear—"Arthur under orders from the Governor of Singapore to go back because he belonged to the army volunteers. So when she told me she was going to have her first baby we were terribly upset." having babies, washing nappies, learning how to cook on rations. "I never washed a cup and saucer til I was twenty. Never washed a handkerchief, never washed a pair of stockings. We weren't burdened at all with the worries that young people have today."

did they burn coal in that house in Melbourne? smell of damp linen, of coal ash, of kerosene on the asphalt outside. "You don't see the young ones going about looking terribly happy." a marsh, a pool, the remains of a great house. "Leaving school and wondering if they're going to get jobs, wondering what's before them."

my aunt removing the dinner dishes:

"I can remember reading the *Dandy* when I was kneehigh to a grass-hopper and thinking it was terribly funny when this chap was awarded a medal but they hadn't got a medal so they gave him a razorblade for shaving gooseberries."

calling them up

Ring O' Bells on the square, Free House Basket Meal—Chips &
Sausages or Fish (plaice, cod, halibut), not free, next door to The
Tinner's Rabbits, tinners having long since sloped elsewhere, asleep in
Loving Memory Of. slate roof, lych gate, foxglove & red campion
hedges.

"their telephones purr," he points to the kiosk. *Lift receiver, Listen for
continuous purring.*

Horatio, Gabriel, Gideon, Faith. lots of Sarahs enduring on. Holmes,
Weakes, Webber, Thorn all gone. departed Chagford's public square,
its tourist eyes, its itinerant "priceless"—*Historic, See in Bus Shelter*—
cameras & cornets & ices.

When you hear rapid pips—"sounds like an old man burping"—*press in
coin*—holding the receiver to his ear. recording it all to play back
home.

i think of them downing their share of Harvest Bitter with its promised
ears of corn, taking Courage from The Gold Rooster & that golden egg
somehow forever in the future. what lies elsewhere has been used up.
what shines in the hedge is only film wrapper.

driving Dartmoor hills

we come climbing, through Ashburton where bright flags are flying &
houses all pastel colours front narrow streets, through woods &
meadow iris, up past stonewalled enclosures Dartmoor ponies roam,
not wild no, though furry, to Widecombe with its wagonroof church,
its yew tree they hung bounty animals from, fox & badger, dance in the
wind off the common, church spire kicked by the Devil's horse—one
cardsharp carried off forever napping.

"Old Uncle Tom Cobley & all" my uncle sings through open windows
of his car escaping "all along, down along, out along lee," the old grey
mare "a-making her will," these wilful tensions twisted in the blood
familial. fried banana-&-cheese sandwiches & silence. sent to Coven-
try for bad behaviour, brooding under the shadow of the wild grey
mère, who never should have had children he says, deleting himself &
my mother from the text of the day. equine temper lashing out, hooves
flashing—sudden slap when the words get unbearable. to overrule
dissent, at all costs maintain the upward climb to a tenuous authority,
star dome & the black winds wild & free. or is it the panic of solitude,
meaningless as stars in empty heaven, as lost, on the night-mare.

"rethinking God now homo erectus has been found to go back 2
million years, & yet," he formulates, turning the wheel, furious, driven,
"at His doorstep I lay certain unexplained events." who writes the text?
who directs this masque?

Hexworthy: smattering of houses in a twisty combe, a clapper bridge. i
take their two heads in front of blue sky, my uncle showing his hand,
my son reading diamonds, clubs where words were, some kingfisher,
was it Wonderboy disappearing under a rock age three in the arms of
his Indian ayah, Mary with the rosary always in her hands. how she
loved him she said, how far away from Bombay England was—as far as
moon from earth, this motorway from the path to the rocks, from the

spring with its temple flowers gone yellow & brown for the spirit of streaming. She will swallow you up if you cannot admit Her, name Her— "most impossible at full moon." notes a shift to the shadow, *märe*, moon sea, when even the eyes change colour, month of oak in England looking two ways. spanning two worlds.

small man on a tor, looking for miles & the sea almost within view, turn full circle in the wind, recalling snow, mist. "imperious & unpredictable . . . " the moor is where you come to get lost, the mysterious moor with its mire at Fox Tor, with its ghosts. "& feeling sorry for herself . . . "

"I always came first with Grandpa & your mother. I always want to come first with people"—mauve & blue, she tells the story from her point of view, how else? "queening it around the lodge," he says. star of a shattered system of domestics, memorial orbits of love, spasmodic, reaching far back in the blood—where there is a gap, a black hole somewhere.

leaning out on twilight rolling in on Dartmoor hills:

to be free, have scope, do what you like, go at large, feel at home, stand
on your rights

to feel at home, even on unfamiliar ground, stand on your own (two
feet, two eyes, ears, nose, ten tactile fingers go where the wind goes . . .

be unnamed,
walk unwritten, de-scripted, un-described. or else compose, make it say
itself, make it up.

boy with tape recorder
stalking horses in a field of cows:

"here we are in the jungle to stalk & capture some wild animals. let's see what's about. watch out for poisonous snakes too. ah ha! i have spotted some Wild Cows & Wild Horses. quick, rope & brand 'em. there they are yonder. they're trying to make a dash for it! (pick pock, pick pock) alright, they haven't seen me yet quite—quite yet. here comes a Wild Horse ! i'd better be careful. i'm lucky i have my revolver. & here comes the rest of the band. watch out you guys, there's a Wild Horse in there."

"ah, she's wild all right."

"he sure is. uh oh there's two of them coming right for us. what should i do? should i shoot them?"

"shoot them?!"

"what else would you do on this jungle safari?"

"you shoot my best mare & you're in trouble."

"they don't think it's very funny. watch out! they're coming right for you guys! aaAGH! oh. they're gone. now join Adventurous Marlatt in his new Adventures with his companion Brownie. hello Brownie, good Brownie. so what will his next adventure be? always on the Safari, always having to fight Wild Animals."

Nattadon Farm

"go on out by the fence & halfway down the field you'll see their holes, big heaps on the ground, they're very clean animals, the badger, 'cause they'll clean out their holes every day. if you stand very still you might spot one coming up for a bit of air."

staring at badger mounds as it grows dark around me on the moor, a few stars appear (no moon), a distant bleating sound of sheep, bird flying, rhythm of horses munching in the next field, & in mine (not mine but theirs) sheep like boulders transfixed staring me down. it isn't badgers i am waiting for.

as commonly told:

poisonous snakes are underground are they?
mmm?
poisonous snakes are underground?
on the ground, yes.
they're not out are they?
mmm?
the snakes!
where?
underground or on the ground?
on the ground. they're not underground.
they're not?
they crawl around, they bite you.

barefoot on the common above cow pasture rising steeply crowned by
free land high above Chagford village, free to dance, sing, yell, cows
low in the distance, cock crow, others in church or asleep in the sun of
a chanted hour & us flying high, high on the wind—play tag with me!
swift or slow, furze burrs in my soul, so high sounds rise with the living
exhalations of the earth we leap from, sallow green smell, flick flick,
are there snakes here mom? momentary in a studied repartee with dogs
nearby, howl for howl, owl for owl answer, only it's roosters crowing
from so far unreeling shouts on the risen air, unreal, their call from
stone walls mingling in the upper nowhere, Nattadon, a name for
nothing but the intersecting colloquy locates us on a rolling map of
moor—animate natter, insect badinage, skin slither

                                               —redbrown
markings on the two sleeping together in a hole in a sunny wall where
my grandmother went to tie her shoe, or was going to, & i pulled her
back saying look! she tells me now, "& they were adders. I didn't want
to frighten you so I only said, my *dear!*"

                                        —adder's tongue, any of several
ferns having a single sterile frond & a long stalk. adder's mouth,

because these small greenish orchids resemble the open mouth of a
snake, *naedre, a naddre*, mistaken for an adder.

watch for adders they said on the moor. only wild rabbit turds, not
even rabbits *on the old gold* . . . he dives into bracken as VENTURE
rides up sweatshirt loud, trots out the word for us in her grey cord
riding helmet, long blonde hair alive in the air—the drift, wide of our
standing still point on a hill, dog yip, crow caw, grass flick wild in the
spoken world.

six years earlier in Vancouver
the English medium began:

"i've just come round that part of the coast of England & i'm
looking . . . & the link is there. thank you."

"do you understand this please? her passing was swift, so swift. you
mother loved birds. as i was talking i saw the swift, you know the swift
of England? a 'blue' bird."

"you know, your grandfather stood tall but your mother stood small in
him. he's protecting her, he's brought her through the ether to you . . .
she is unsteady on her feet . . . she has a musical voice."

"she said it was wonderful. she's telling me . . . & as she turned around,
& she said she fell, she bowled over, but as she looked up she said it
was her father, her father picked her up. & she said it didn't matter, it
didn't matter at all, i only knew he was there. she says don't cry, no
regrets, it couldn't have happened better. something that i dreaded for
so long caught me unawares. because, sweetheart—did she call you
sweetheart? suddenly she said that i was walking down an English lane
with my father. you couldn't be unhappy with that, could you now?
because she has the memory of an English lane & she also has the
memory of a very old English church, at the right hand side of the lane
going down to it, i can hear, let him describe, *is all the battle won.* &
unity, the cause of unity. there are an awful lot of her people over there
'cause she walked into the church to meet them, your father took her
into the church & they were all there. he said—that was your grandfather—that's one way of getting them all together & you don't have to
buy them drinks."

3. Burning into Blue

June 22, Ilfracombe, Combe Martin where i stayed as a child—bits of intact memory but the overall terrain is different, filled in now on the map

"bracing sea air," homeopathic pills, allergens

meanwhile the Middle East

shops full of water wings, inflatable rings, & spades for digging up things

June 24, Ellesmere. B & B—Mrs. E., our "prop." tells me poppies have died out in English cornfields because of weed-killer

to Ilfracombe

from Barnstaple market town, the River Taw tidepull & ebb along
sand shone by sea, by sky, high up & thrilled with it to Ilfracombe. a
doubledecker sway away, at the top, in the front, a woman in her
summerdress wellfilled, her boy & girl replete with comics & toffee, &
she? from her purse she pulls a doll, idly combing its hair its mermaid
smile hers, unasked, uncalled for *souvenir*—her son catches it & turns
away.

mine is intrigued with them silly on the sunny side in blue, dresses &
navy blazers stretched with hysteria, they scream kneeling on their
seats mugging the bus behind, you never! oh come *on*! sun fills everyone even the withered shopper, full o' beans all right, i'll say, as we
stick outside the George with its Whitbread sign, rush hour in
Braunton, i could do with a drop o' that. everything calls, shines,
points to itself.

on our way past slopes, streams, yellow flag, blue tractor with a red L,
winding above Woolacombe strand white below, up the headland our
road reflecting curves in windowglass opposite from the trees we go, fog
blowing up off the edge to crest at Mullacott: caravans, fields of
threshed hay, raked, unraked, stacked, yellow squares in the round
green of folds sinking into other rolls, curves, down on down we
descend, to Ilfracombe.

o gingerbread hotels i know you, palms growing on the Channel, bed
& breakfast with your antimacassars, marmalade & HP sauce. damp
loos with medicinal TP, your quay with the seaman's chapel perilous,
your lettered flowerbeds & crowns, Ilfracombe, penny arcades with the
Digger, the Gypsy Fortuneteller, the Haunted Bed-Chamber—Spirits
Play a Prominent Part in Jinks Adventures. *this* is the adventure, & the
familiar, strangely dislocated, bits & pieces of a town to be put together
from a geography that doesn't quite fit, living on in spirit. what it was,

only, ever, the beady eye of Moira & her finger falling, there, on the line that says, that stops, *rewind*. & the penny falling into its slot forever.

Combe Martin

let off the bus with our bags & pack & where shall we go? here at the heart of what i remember of Combe Martin, curve of Seaside Hill running down to the cove where tide daily climbs the shingle beach to a seawall clutter of small hotels, new plate glass fish & chip place, shops of High Street stretching back up the combe. let's eat, he says. somewhere along there my grandparents lived. somewhere along here we stayed (where the fish & chip place is? come on!) at the heart of an absence—father sailing for Canada. mother sisters & me in a guesthouse perched like gulls on the rocks a few weeks before we leave.

no, we rolled like stones & she was the gull. unsettled, sad. we wanted to shout, we're going to Canada aren't we? she was alone & we rolled blithely down Cobbler's Hill, patted strange dogs, bickered for ices, wandered off. *you scream & icescream*—screaming with laughter.

my grandfather talked about strain & cracking. my grandmother had us pick gooseberries, red currents, walked us to Sunday School. where was she? Tino, my mother, small in a henge of emotion, removed somewhere. no stars to plot this course, only foreboding & hope against her father's words, against the script. learning how to fly.

Guest House, 1951

in wellingtons & red rubber raincape begrudging, trudging up Seaside
Hill. ugly trailing behind the flock, come on, get a move on, not even
wanting to be where the stupid seagulls swoop flat sea, nagging, shrieky
yawps of outrage. boots too big. hot cape pulling drawstring tight round
face dripping nose down lip, scratchy. hands nestled inside their slits at
least dry won't even lift one to help myself, will be, the walking
mummy wrapt in rubber, resent (well) (meant) dumb obliged.

& that was nine, that was the line connecting me with this narrowing
pavement, how you have to step down into the road still to pass
someone, stone wall, guest house on the hill, ruled by a tyrant prop. my
mother, guest, tyrannical for walks against high-jinks, high energy
herself afraid of—who? & Mrs. Who will be annoyed at you, running
the hall, sliding down bannisters, don't slam that door. i'm disappointed in you, the oldest, you ought to know better.

knowing nothing of tyrannosaurus (we don't usually accept children)
teeth bared, "smile." knowing something of sovereign power, & of
resistance (foot dragging)—the line running back to my mother's
father who fed me vocabulary along with the meloids he used to suck,
black-tongued, small, dry-humoured Grandpa, slipping me keys to
doors he had shut.

naptime & the doors closed. supposed to be sleeping, let's play circus,
tying the cords of our blue dressinggowns to form a tightrope between
two giant wardrobes which, with a little weight applied (o acrobat of
imagination, o tutu spangled highwire star) crash dangerously toward
each other, stop, just, over my unsmashed sisters crying. mother
furiously unable to budge, get your grandfather—& run. down High
Street, furies of disaster after. my grandmother: o lord, he's playing
billiards—confused with bilious (looking bilious, dear) a word i knew
meant castor oil or worse—i deserved worse, Grandpa huffing &
puffing up the stairs after.

Combe Martin, house martin, Martinmas, Saint Martin, martial swords & plowshares

this earth hospitable, *comfortably furnished. you can sit quietly listening to the movement of a nearby trout stream at the bottom of the garden.* at the bottom of Combe Martin. *steep cliffs, ideal for rambles.* coves with caves, slits, & what lies buried, treasure i told him, *trouvaille* of words rustling, seaweed, looking for minnows & crabs in tidal pools the rocks have caught back from the sea. in sandals, *sandalie*, the shoe of a Lydian god i buy him in a shop on High Street full of boxes. no cape, nothing else to change into in the phone kiosk.

nowhere to fly to but here, where even the grass makes him sneeze, June the worst month for pollen count. happiest in the Lucky Penny counting hits or testing quickness of eye against sci fi enemy bombers in Japanese computer games. divine wind recycled (on & on). while in Chatham they sing the Navy Blues, *getting rid of us at a high rate of knots* (outmoded). Nott planning to plug the Faroe gap with *nuclear-powered killer submarines & radar-equipped reconnaissance aircraft.* (getting rid of us.) while here small boats chug out to sea in the mist with a boatload of eyes, no sign of fish, a shark she said, lashed bleeding to the post on the beach in old revenge.

postwar turned prewar words return, swallows in the light: ices & Flook (luck invisible), chip shops spawning B & B's, prim Ellesmere & Frittiscombe, Redlap, Merrymeet pristine even. *oldfashioned comfort is the rule. she brought us tea in the evening,* her husband a member of the Auxiliary Coast Guard sees what the Concorde does to the wind, flying overhead as it passes its twin from Bristol, wind rushing in to fill the vacuum of their passing, split & blown in 2 opposite directions at once. this is the image of the end, my landlady says, *wars & the rumour of wars. having forgot the sign of the fish,* she says, the, the, pointing to fix us in forever, how the meek shall inherit the earth meaning uncorrupt this body, even now *it is written, Our flesh shall slumber in the ground Till*

the last trumpets joyful sound—sounding Creeks & Loverings & Berrys
buried deep in small earth mounds, tombs, tumescent upthrust womb
waiting.

& in owl light, twi-light, listen—where is my grandmother hiding out,
cooking fish kedgeree off High Street? setting her foot with its golfing
shoe untied on a sunny stone: look, Giggi, 2 snakes sleeping together. o
my dear, she whispered, jumping back. o more than luck—grace,
wingtip, brushed now by it in its turning. what does a child know? not
The Truth That Leads to Eternal Life, my landlady handing it to me gift-
wrapped. not there the light, flash, buried deep & inarticulate as earth.

perched on the rocks, birdlike, picking over small life in tidal pools,
dead crabs floating by, or live & gone from the hand, i see my ghostly
child in him, not gone & not quite him, as she in me, mother, grandmother, grand, full grown we stand in, not for. that earth takes back
what is given, *ghos-ti*, hostly & hostile at once. *guests will be provided
with a hot water bottle,* immaculately shining bath, long boat, long
barrow at the end of the day's rambles.

Climbing the Hangman

"alternate route"

Little or Great (steep), rise with the
gulls, morning, past cowpies, swishing
tails, stiles, thick briar & foxglove,
ear deafened, (ab)surd weight to earth,
almost under sun's beam stone—

wait, atop this round head, live coal,
ember, breathe, ardent into blue, wing
tipt & light fleshed

Ellesmere

such tides of feeling—grey despair even, listening to Kit coughing through the door in fits, attacks. how can he be allergic to the very grass?

he misses joking around with my cousins. i'm too serious, sitting on the staircase waiting for him to fall asleep, worrying. can hear the telly going in the other room, the news confirm my landlady's view of history, this plot we're in . . .

stairs painted white under a familiar-beige carpet. lace at the window. pot of plastic anemones & one liquor bottle, one jamjar, one picklejar full of tinted water. small histories.

what if history is simply the shell we exude for a place to live in? *all wrapped up*. break out before it buries us. stories can kill.

it's the amusement arcade that holds him, as it once held me, though it isn't Moira or the repeated opening of a coffin that fascinates (they aren't even there with their creaking mechanical magic). now it's electronic hand-eye, faster than a speeding bullet, the plotted line the hand selects, *selects*, eye impressed with target accuracy, ears full of hit-noise. sneezing uncalled-for in that world & hence forgotten.

Stories hold in
~ open art

Lynmouth, mouth of the Lyn, mouth of the precipice

I don't remember being here before, Lynton, Lynmouth, met by a cliff
the funicular railway descends, gush of water building up to slow &
steady drop through trees, under footbridge, over eaves we slide &
brake our way down past that counterweight of curious faces & bodies
leaning out to look halfway. between fun & funicular, a cable, small
rope on which our lives depend.

there will be rain, if clover stands upright, if scarlet pimpernel should
close, poor man's weatherglass. *exit, pursued by mullahs.* seeing, as it is,
wind veer uneasy between hoardings he enjoys the puff of something
junked, by the old pump station, some antique—let's go. later. history
as Mme. Tussaud's. what is it about a crowd of faces stepped, descend-
ing, inside time, or mossed-up concrete, water, looking up? *a stand-off
in the war.* he hands us two punched tickets. "what for?" so we feel
we're taking a trip, down, herded or heralded. could be the cablecar up
Penang Hill i want him to see. back there, then. or me at his age?
before eyes, his, were even conceived i carried their possibility. playing
with tickets, play traffic lights to go, go, stop. beyond even the image of
event—outcome, issuance. the cold light of tomorrow.

i don't remember this rivermouth, cloud rolling in, this shape the
village takes along its banks, taking place to be the meeting, Lyn east,
west, Lyn (ravine). we climb a wood anxious signs warning us *gorge,
weir, steep incline, hold small children by the hand.* these domesticated
woods hung with one idea there might never be a *crisis-free environ-
ment,* appalled reason daily posting evidence.

he isn't interested in the fall of trees or even houses, village sliding out
the mouth of the Lyn into the sea. he isn't interested in the Valley of
the Rocks, heathland, uncultivated stone walls & stands of ancient
culture knew its stone womb. he isn't interested & maybe i wasn't &

don't remember being hauled up the Gorge to see the waterfall which later & before us now came down on their sleeping heads.

whether the moon on its back holds the rain in its lap or a full moon clears the sky, our weather now internally defined with these extensions of our hands, & by ours—something is gone from the day. *I remember it . . . as a day on which the sun did not really shine (again) & the wind blew south-westerly, Force 6. But by the year 2000 hardly anything other than the Israeli attack will be attached to that particular date.* horizon folds in on us, whole cloudracks floating in so bikers' helmets sitting eyeless on the wall of the esplanade against grey sky recapitulate storm warning signals darker. only when we ascend ordering pizza & omelette in this small bistro on a winding street, does it begin, dread, *draedan*, pain that grabs him in the right shoulder. "what is it?" "i feel like Alien's trying to be born out of me."

& rushes to the men's while i sit locked in helplessness. & when the man at the next table gets back he says he is outside in the garden, he seems all right. out there in another light, knowing what to do.

Ellesmere, Combe Martin

what was it? besides Alien he thought he was having a heart attack (in his shoulder?) but it was on the wrong side. a muscle spasm? he was himself again so fast. it fills me with dread & not for the first time. i think how can we be here for another two weeks. i only want to fly home with him, to keep him safe. where does this feeling come from that i have put him at risk? that the longer we stay here the more i tempt fate?

close to the edge

in caves. she is in caves. but i don't feel her here. along the causeway, light bouncing brilliants off housefronts, evening strollers, off waves to the Dolphin, Fo'c'sle, off the Royal Marine—*we get our storms here.* she is not here, if anywhere, past cliffs to Wild Pear Beach where darkness gathers in cracks, slits, tidal caverns, gathering us up (& fascinated, wanting to go back in all the way, nose up against those walls of rock, musty with sea rank pebbles, sea-wrack fear of old, being trapt by the sea) she said the tide is coming up, if we don't go now we won't get back & i could hear it in her, panic, pan-ic (terror of the wild), shouldn't have brought you here, all three, & the wind rising—risk. to meet it.

hand-hold & scramble-hold, strong fingers on rock climb up & over, despite short pleated frocks, despite the *irresponsible, incapable,* hammers in her head—panting at the top, exhilarated, we did it.

taking us close to the edge, over & over.

we did, in the end, as she asked, on a different sea-coast off a different rock, lean from the boat to scatter bits of porous bone, fine ash. words were not enough. & the sea took her.

4. Trains of Thought

June 26. we almost missed our stop playing gin-rummy

June 27. next through train? not on Saturday

on the train

the unexpected. *thunder & lightning* gets served up on a plate as treacle tart with clotted cream. he slides back into his seat, flushed, do you want to hear my dream?

we had this big giant house, right? & it's really a weird-looking house, you see, because inside they had long hallways & big square rooms like your aunt's house. (they? well you, or whoever. we were living there only it was in our neighbourhood.) i was a guy that would get clubs together, something like that, & so i went to the Housing Project— well i didn't *go* there 'cause i was too scared, but there were these homeless kids, a bunch of them, six, five, four, small like that, & i took them back with me to let them sleep in our backyard—are you writing this down? (yes, don't say it so fast.) so i was in the house in my best-looking uniform 'cause i was really happy & my friend & secretary whose name was Mark, he comes over to me & says hey Kit, there's a gang, sorta like a group of kids who're wearing the same colour uniform in a lineup outside the windows like in a procession, & these guys were in blue uniform (are you making this up as you go along? i'm telling it to you like it *was*.) & Mark goes, there's a group out there so i walk over to the window & open it a bit & they are saying idol, idol, idol in rhythm & i raise my hands like saying please, you're too kind, & they said, we're doing that to make you in a good mood to talk to us, we've got something to complain about. i looked outside the window looking further left & there was a whole bunch of groups there—it seemed our backyard was very long—so i got down on my hands & knees, i didn't talk to that group after i saw all the other groups, & i crawled down this long hallway under the windows—we had a lot of windows in that house—so nobody could see me. when i got close to each window the noise was loud saying where are you? come on, we know you're in there, & when i went past the window it would fade away. & then i got to a room that was small & compact like B's room & i tried to creep up to the window & look out of it without people seeing me.

outside i spotted a bunch of teenagers hanging around the steps next door smoking pot & drinking beer but they spotted me. i was really feeling cool then but i knew it was stupid for they said, hey look it's the king, hi Kit be praised. & so i took up my courage & said very modestly, what're you doing there on those steps? you're supposed to ask Jack. it's your lawn you said, & you let those homeless kids stay—i looked over at the kids by the window, all six of them were huddled together & staring about them in scaredness & amazement—so we decided we'd stay, after all you said it was a free world. (as if it were, free—to turn, this not so free—as if you'd *said*.)

what i should've told about earlier was all the people in the yard. they all did the same thing the teenagers did & the teenagers were mean street kids. there were tons of them. there were small kids playing tag & ten-year-olds watching their portable tv on the lawn. there were also tourists sitting on their deckchairs getting suntanned. (— Lynmouth. place here overlays there, home (dream overlay) "home free," free to be—what?)

my parents were having their normal arguments at suppertime. they were slipping tapes (they? well you, only it was only part of you. me that is part of us in relation to him is them. is fiction then? but me 'n him are in a narrative train going someplace we don't even recognize) slipping tapes with their arguments into each other's chairs & beds & books. they'd always use the same tape, listen to it, & tape their message over it. the dumb thing was though they didn't listen very good & when they recorded their message they weren't really thinking about it, they were just letting loose their anger. (hearing out this train of thought, the dream, is recognizing the terrain.) our company for tonight was my aunt & my favourite cousin & they were all talkative. i was very pissed off about this. outside the cheering came loud & clear, the king! the king! where's that false king? & then a voice came, hey come outa there you chicken! i wasn't that scared 'cause i was so angry. in a rage i stomped downstairs to the door which was sorta like in the basement but it wasn't *in* the basement, it was on the level. i flung open the door & glared at them. they just glared back. i've had it up to here with you jerk-offs i said, especially you teenagers, my parents are about to split up, we've got company that i'm not ready for, & i've got *you*—jeez. they all stopped talking. you know, you're all fucked up, i said catching my cool. i only let those kids stay here 'cause they're homeless. you're not homeless so clear off. some of them started to get up & leave & then some more . . .

sitting face to face across a moving table, recognizing our difference.

if it wasn't for the clouds England wouldn't be so green, you see, it would be all dry grass now wouldn't it?

windswept. tearing down the Motorway in a private Mini driven by a tallkneed blacksuited Rail official, we are kindly being returned to point of departure having got off the wrong train. no place in England he says more than seventy miles from the sea.

he means you can't really get lost. lucky you ran into the boss. the man with the bowler hat & pocket watch on a chain? the same. he's the area manager, he's responsible for everything coming in on time. tucked us under his brim, regarded us as guests, misguided, maladressed. you were heading for Penzance you know. dropped from the train at Newbury Racecourse like two tickets tossed into a ditch except it was flat as the prairies, strong wind blowing & nothing to hold us down but the empty staircase over the tracks, a distant clutter of Rail officials conferring, confirming, disapprobation, summer in Antarctic & nowhere for the pendragon ship, here she comes, the next train won't be by for an hour yet, & British standards high he tucked us into a yellow Mini & sent us back.

5. Black Hole at Centre

June 28, Pilgrim Cottage. the ex-governor & his lady, simply Jean & Nick growing old together in a cottage in the Cotswolds

"doing the right thing?"

June 30. circling the power thresholds of Stonehenge—embracing the squat stone mothers of Avebury

under her mothering wing

five thousand year old long barrow bones planted like seeds in the ground— they cultivated death to ensure a new spring

our culture trades in death—big business arms race

cottage in the Cotswolds

like walking into *the very picture of* . . .

slate roof, roses twining up the stone wall to the eavestrough, *delphiniums blue*, larkspur & lupins in the honeyed light. Nick on his knees among the cabbage (evening relief from a desk of government papers) or walking with the gait of a man who savours growing things.

Jean recalling a government reception in Sarawak, dancing with Nick aboard ship for Malaysia, while her hands rinse garden lettuce, shake the crinkles out of sundried linen. explain energy conservation in a knight's house. explain digging the garden or washing the clothes yourself. this is very English.

i feel lost. layer on layer of place, person. dramatis personae. the nameless creature i am at the heart of this many-chambered shell is getting overlaid, buried under. coming down with a cold? Kit coughs his way through the night restless as if the room were packed with dream people, dream words.

Pilgrim Cottage

not even tai chi helps on the rollered lawn. day dawns blue & surreal. i am insulated by a stuffed-up nose, aching head. Kit wants only to curl by the fire, dormouse-like, with the "activity box" Jean unearthed. have we come all this way to be mothered? (my head stuffed with unwept tears?)

she is the gate-keeper. tall, sane, with a body mine resembles much more than my mother's. childless, she is my mother's closest school friend, whose memory i've come to trace, who was there in the inner-most circle—(she says it isn't Stonehenge i must visit but Avebury).

Jean with the carrying voice (the same recitation class my mother took?). Jean who has trimmed her lamp to "sensible," that kudos earned by the oldest. as i am one. as my mother was—barely. my mother more an only or lonely one, stripped of her brother, of her parents another world away, left for seven years in boarding school (who gets to write the text?), "always imagining the worst."

Jean describes my mother's "anti-" nature, that puzzle. the resister, antagonizer, the one who never "fitted in." how she "seemed to enjoy setting people against her"—a noncompliance Jean admired, being the dutiful daughter, easily guilted.

(as i am torn between? my rebel bound to the dutiful one? Jean remem-bers me "the perfect little mother" as a child. o the weariness of Weirfield school morality, passed on, passed on.)

antagonist that other child-mother, my mother: whose image comes clear. hating the headmistress, hating to spend holidays at school when everyone else had gone home. (how far away from Bombay, from Malacca England was then.) loving scripture & literature, hating to have to learn the wars of history when she wanted to dream (see

"romanticize"). hiding in the boiler room to read novels, escape
hockey. walking in crocodiles to morning services, being short &
having to walk at the end. "over-dramatizing," saying how much the
teachers hated her when according to Jean they didn't hate her at all.

or they hated what was subversive in her: imagination, that *mad
boarder in the house of the mind, which alone can prevent a house from
being built on safe, practical & boring foundations* (Sagan). that winged
thing that flies off the handle, leaps out the window . . .

she who had her wings clipped growing up: wondering even as a
mother was she "doing the right thing"? hiding her doubts to wrestle
with the angel authority of father, teacher, doctor, dentist, priest.
furious, raging at the false front of society, tearing out the placid
assumptions of family . . . & then lapsing, controlled, into silence.

avenging abdication, you said i would be sorry when you were dead, &
i only understood it as a curse.

Pilgrim Cottage still

i am struggling as if by reflex, as if i can do nothing else.

i argue with Jean, irritated by her sense of duty, even as i am grateful
for the way she looks after us. Kit woke with a fever, stomach ache this
morning & she immediately got us an appointment with her doctor. a
virus, i was told, nothing serious. antibiotic to keep his chest clear.
picked up at the nearest chemist's—full of the smell of disinfectant &
drugs, of patient grave faces waiting on expert opinion.

he is flushed & limp. i feel alarm rush through me like wings. mother
hen, my mother would say. brooding. as if there were some evil i
struggle against.

i look up evil in the dictionary, *ubilaz*, exceeding the proper limit. what
is "the limit"? for either the dead or the living?

delphiniums blue & geraniums red

rose light in the blue, at eye level (where is the dormouse curled?) their
kitchen looks out on where it suffuses hayfield, appletree, vegetable-
garden hedge—day's amber, stilled & stilling. watch fresh lettuce
leaves, curled, disappear in the spinner. watch a child, curled up in
himself for comfort, dreaming of blue. roselight makes of their kitchen
unearthly hue, seraphic even, in our vision blue, is a healing colour
even a bird will spring toward.

but i was blue with cold on the Didcot Platform in a wind the intercity
diesels roar on through. torn holes in attention. out of nowhere we are
near the source. a shallow brook ripples by a few crosses at fords, a few
stone walls for leaning up against—the Thames, really? not that one.
wellspring. dayspring. home—when the walls come down, what kind of
source?

that was Old Bernie, she said, on his last legs waiting outside surgery
with his stick, "they're all full up in there"—refused the chair she
offered to fetch from the grocer's. no relief from the blinking exit sign:
alone & knowing it.

despite all this pulling together. Taunton, Weirfield. running out on
the hockey team blue with cold, "you can't be cold." grown older,
painting the open wound with iodine, "it doesn't hurt, it's for your own
good really." slogans on the road to selfless, sightless in the guise of
ought-to-be—chrysanthemums, say, on the unclipped village graves.
when *five-year-olds* (are) *looting burned-out shops* "these days of career
marchers & young punks tearing up the streets. it's all me-me, no sense
of the common good, now have they?"

& if The Common Good, pointing its nineteenth century hand, has
tyrannized all sense of me, small voice essential to life? so that we falls
apart, gone mad at the mask of Reason which still is quoting Good in

the face of annihilation: tactical advantage, counterforce capability, stockpiling. *the first few weapons arriving do almost all the damage conceivable to the fabric of the country.* have done so, without ever arriving, the nest we live in full of holes these days.

& still: *i suppose all these people know better than i*—doubtful, paws to eyes, small creature at the heart of dreaming some blue otherwhere. *& that is the reason,* the story continues, circling back to its source, that the dormouse curls, imagining delphiniums blue, o blue/black hole at centre, folding in on itself.

Pilgrim night

the terror of being, alone on your own in the dark. the terror of
dragging your child along in the panic woods in the night crying,
having a child when you *are* a child—terror a kind of trembling in the
heart, helpless, listening to him cough. he coughed so much he
couldn't catch his breath, heart pounding, & very hot.

this morning he threw up, over & over. phoned the doctor who said
take him off every medication, he must be allergic. altered reaction.
what altered it?

there is no limit. something in me is in shock, like a bird beating wildly
against a branch—lost, panicked. why are we going through this?

just noticed him shallow breathing with eyes half open. went over to
stroke his forehead, ask if he was cold. as he focussed his eyes (coming
back? from where?) he said no, scared, scared of being sick. (me too.)
but i said, try to think strong thoughts & sleep, your body can heal
itself while you sleep. i say the mother-things to him but what do i say
to the child in me? who mothers me?

long after The Brown Day of Bride

her tomb-body . . . built to contain that primary chaos, long barrow of
bones, dismembered or not, of potsherds, all mingled together.

winter, this time of the year, submerged. as i am, heavy with cold. on
the other side "down under" watching almond blossom in the chill
streets of their world. a place to visit, blurring distinction between
corpus & corpse.

quick, running to meet them, with pots, meat bones, flint implements,
with stone, bone & shell beads. rubbish, *from which new life annually
rises,*

cup-&-ring, stone ring within a ring, the Farmer's in the Dell (is that
you, Bride of the Brown Day, of the White Hills?)

& we all pat the bone, thinking to make it ring us round, earth word
(home again), seed word (safe again),

                              that bears us in this *kiel,* to
ku-, to, a hollow space or place, enclosing object, round object, a lump.
mound in the surrounding sea of grass. *ku-, kunte,* to, wave-breaking
womb: Bride who comes unsung in the muse-ship shared with Mary
Gypsy, Mary of Egypt, Miriam, Marianne suppressed, become/Mary of
the Blue Veil, Sea Lamb sifting sand & dust, dust & bone, whose
Son . . .

continued

. . . that is the limit of the old story, its ruined circle, that is not how it ended or we have forgotten parts, we have lost sense of the whole. left with a script that continues to write our parts in the passion we find ourselves enacting, old wrongs, old sacrifices. & the endless struggle to redeem them, or them in ourselves, our "selves" our inheritance of words. wanting to make us new again: to speak what isn't spoken, even with all the words.

although there are stories about her, versions of history that are versions of her, & though she comes in many guises she is not a person, she is what we come through to & what we come out of, ground & source. the space after the colon, the pause (between the words) of all possible relation.

Avebury *awi-spek*, winged from buried (egg

nose stuffed eyes holes in the chalk ridge of sinal bones rushed down
back roads' upland grass wind weaving snakelike through. old English
words: the land, the land. man's *life like the life of cereals*. woman's too.

bring to this place the line of a life (palm says it), motive in currents of
changing weather, angst, cold for this time of year

—& small, toy pistol in one hand, cupped, & sheltered by the pelvic
thrust of rock, jumps, gotcha mom!

                     as if to fix it (sine), that jubilant
ego in the face of stone, of wind flocking grey wethers *still gathered like*
(but not the same, not these) sarsens now in place, immutable from
long time back. & front, weathered yes, in folds acquiring character we
read in, clothed & prickling now along the hairless spine, a line
meeting a circle, two in one so huge (small hill) barely visible at grass
view, red windbreaker fleck a sea of green & climb some moat in his
imagination scaled he calls me to: come & get me

    the, all-powerful tickle, gulp, wriggle gulping in the whole world
hugged in ecstatic limit, breath's. nothing still, no duration now (a
line) creeps through fields of (waves of) renewed green, cloud, light.

what was it they got? craniums & long bones in long barrows, construction tools from 4000 years back, *antler picks, rakes, & some ox
shoulderblade shovels*. what perspective from that elevation? *matrix of
chalk block walls arranged in the pattern of a spider's web* around & over a
mound of turves, *grass still pliable though brown in colour . . . beetles . . .
flying ants with their wings* showed them buried late July of 2660 B.C.
why?

the line hypothesized druid lore (in Christian times), today a collective
need to endure winter to spring, when *from his knoll…/ the Serpent will
come from his hole/ on the Brown Day of Bride*, singing, wave on wave
emerging: & at centre, earth, only earth.

narrative is a strategy for survival. so it goes—transformative sinuous
sentence emerging even circular, cyclic Avebury, April-May leaps
winged from *buried*. sheds lives, laps, folds, these identities, sine: fold of
a garment/ chord of an arc (active misreading). writing in monumental
stones, open, not even capstone or sill, to sky (-change). *she lives* stands
for nothing but this longstanding matter in the grass, settled hunks of
mother crust, early Tertiary, bearing the rootholes of palms. they bring
us up, in among stone-folds, to date: the enfolded present waits for us
to have done with hiding-&-seeking terrors, territories, our obsession
with the end of things.

how hug a stone (mother) except nose in to lithic fold, the old slow
pulse beyond word become, under flesh, mutter of stone, *stane, stei-*ing
power.

back to Reading

back to the white stone lady reclined on her stone couch at the foot of the garden at the end of the Empire, in an attitude of elegant attentiveness. what thunder is she listening to? who put her there? a tranquilly attentive point of return in the surreal wash this dream is. Kit seems over his allergy & the dark weight is gone.

we have passed the anniversary of her death, walking up the road in the sweet-smelling night recalling her. he remembers being too small to reach the kitchen counter, he remembers the garden & his "secret passage" through overgrown bushes to the door. he remembers she didn't know what to do with him, the first boy in the family.

i think of the shape of her life, her brooding silence. how i felt i was struggling often with her sense of fatality, either about herself or about us, her children, the struggle with her fear which i suspected of being so strong it could actually shape what happened to me. coming to meet it, i see what i've been struggling with here.

in an atmosphere of war, of riots. the man next door predicts the collapse of the money system, visions of pre-war Germany, Bergman's *The Serpent's Egg* all over again.

& at the heart of this, Kit's rapture at feeding the pigeons. as i photograph him i am the photo of me with my sisters, the same fear & joy, hands outstretched, three of us in velvet-collared coats, mother hovering, en route to Canada, feeding the pigeons in Trafalgar Square.

feeding the pigeons

to speak to, call to (here, pigeon, come on, it's all right) the free &
unobliged (come on, birdies), plastic dish of seed at arm's length so
they fly, flutter, squawk, perch, lift at will in a flash wheeling his
shoulders, aura of feathers falling flaring winged things

not the National Gallery, not the Tate. he wants to be where live
things are soaring past Nelson on his column, over birdshit on the
Imperial Lions, falling rhythm & whorling in great broken rings across
this memorial to war

over the Nile, Cape St. Vincent, over Copenhagen & Trafalgar cast
from captured French cannon . . . over *milk floats & a concrete mixer . . .
(hurled) stones & petrol bombs, vehicles overturned & set alight . . .*
   strong grey wings, stunted claws, some twisted & deformed, one
with wire round its feet (catch it & then we can free it)—panickt
flapping. plump grey breast with green leaves & violets. stand back, if
you don't stand back you'll catch it, taxis whirring by in fleets clipping
the edge off unwary pedestrians looking left. from under her veil she
warns, stand back, if you fall off the edge you'll be electrocuted. as it
begins, this thrum way back in the tunnel rocketing forward, fear,
rocketing through my whole being
      lost
            squat   turbanned hawking   muddy water   boys haul off the
white   ship-leave two hours   Towers of Silence   vultures   welcome to Bombay madam   three small girls ah very pretty   to the zoo
she said knowing it at Parel Road   Victoria & Albert   untouchable
scream in the air tearing like fine silk   how does she know Hindi
know this isn't the way stiffening you will die insane in a foreign
country
            yes yes this is the way   to contact shrinking inside   her
jewellery
            Maha Amba   stop stop i say   beating on the glass with rupees

right here   but mem this is not the zoo   right now it's Mumbai every
cab back a possible abduction off unknown streets to bring us back
do you speak English? do you know the way to the pier?   unbearable
loss don't take them from me

                              her i lost, not him in the throng,
djellabas, saris, japanese sailors, punks with mohican haircuts, honky
Canadians circling the downspout of Empire. he stands in blue joggers
firmly planted on cement. hey mom, look at him on my head, take a
picture, mom, he's the greediest. lost in the behaviour of pigeons,
plump, fast-flying birds with small heads & low cooing voices, domes-
tic & ringtailed, rock-dove alone in the ruined palace crying, *ku? ku?
ku? (qua?)* where have you gone? first love that teaches a possible
world

   —i want to go home, he says, where it's nice & boring. here
everyone's scared deep down. here everyone's forgotten how to laugh.
hearing the grandfather clock tick on . . .

   & i can do nothing but stand in my sandals & jeans unveiled, beat
out the words, dance out names at the heart of where we are lost, hers
first of all, wild mother dancing upon the waves, wide-wandering dove
beat against, & the dance beats with you, claims of the dead in our
world (the fear that binds). i am learning how the small ones live,
ruffled neck feathers ripple snakelike movement of the neck last
vestige of dinosaurs: then lift, this quick wing flap, heart at breast
strike up a wild beating, blood for the climb, glide, rest, on air current,
free we want to be where live things are.